Erec and Enide

Erec and Enide

Chrétien de Troyes

Translated from the Old French by

Burton Raffel

Afterword by Joseph J. Duggan

Yale University Press

New Haven & London

Library of Congress Cataloging-in-Publication Data
Chrétien, de Troyes, 12th cent.
[Erec et Enide. English]
Erec and Enide / Chrétien de Troyes ; translated from the Old French by Burton Raffel ; afterword by Joseph J. Duggan.
p. cm.
Includes bibliographical references.
ISBN 0-300-06770-4 (cloth : alk. paper). — ISBN 0-300-06771-2 (pbk.)
1. Erec (Legendary character)—Romances. 2. Arthurian romances.
I. Raffel, Burton. II. Title.
PQ1445.E6E5 1997
841'.1—dc20 96-35477
CIP

A catalogue record for this book is available from the British Library.

The paper in this book meets the guidelines for permanence and durability of the Committee on Production Guidelines for Book Longevity of the Council on Library Resources.

For Isaac Moses Pride

Contents

Translator's Preface

This is the second of Chrétien's great narratives I have translated. The first, *Yvain,* was published by Yale University Press in 1987. The publishers and I plan, over the next several years, to produce versions of the three remaining poems.

Most of what needs to be explained about the technical aspects of this translation has already been set out, in my Translator's Preface to *Yvain.* And as I also said there, "I will be content if this translation allows the modern English reader some reasonably clear view of Chrétien's swift, clear style, his wonderfully inventive story-telling, his perceptive characterizations and sure-handed dialogue, his racy wit and sly irony, and the vividness with which he evokes, for us his twentieth-century audiences, the emotions and values of a flourishing, vibrant world." I need only add that the longer I work with Chrétien, the more "modern" he seems to me, in virtually all his essential characteristics—which may help to explain why, as I said in concluding that prior translator's preface, "Chrétien is a delight to read—and to translate." Not easy, but definitely a delight.

Although it is perhaps more usual to work from a single version of the text to be translated, I have chosen—for *Erec and Enide* and for the three remaining poems as well—to translate from the two most recent editions of the Old French original, the *Oeuvres complètes* (1994), edited for Gallimard's deservedly famous Pléiade series by Daniel Poirion and five collaborating scholars, *Erec* having been edited by Peter F. Dembowski, and the complete *Romans* (1994), edited for the Le Livre de Poche series, once again, by a team of scholars, *Erec* being edited by Jean-Marie Fritz. Although they have worked with the accumulated scholarship of eight hundred years and have had at their disposal all the tools of contemporary technology, these enormously learned folk have been utterly unable to arrive at a single, solid notion of what Chrétien did and did not write. Accordingly, I have worked with both texts constantly open in front of me, picking and choosing what seemed to me, after years of translating Chrétien, to most accurately represent his style. I have consulted and (of course) shamelessly pillaged the helpful textual, historical, and literary notes in these editions. I mean no disrespect to all those who labored to produce readable modern French prose versions of Chrétien, for both editions, but cannot help noting, finally—with a wry smile that Chrétien might well have echoed—that *neither* of those prose translations seems to me as faithful to, nor as fully representative of, the brilliantly moving poetry of the Old French original as the verse translation that follows.

Université des Acadiens
Lafayette, Louisiana

Erec and Enide

Chrétien de Troyes

Li vilains dit en son respit
Que tel chose a l'an en despit,
Qui mout vaut mieuz que l'en ne cuide.

Peasants have a proverb:
The thing we think worthless
Is worth more than we know.
Work as hard as you can
For wisdom; the sluggard's way
Teaches us, soon enough,
That nothing ventured is nothing
Gained, but something wonderful
Lost. Chrétien, believing
Men should think, and learn,
And use their tongues well,
And teach others, has found
This lovely tale of adventure,
Beautifully put together,
Proving beyond a doubt
That no one granted wisdom
And grace by the mercy of God

Should ever refuse to use it.
He tells of Erec, son
Of Lac—a story professional
Poets usually ruin,
Spinning it out for kings
And counts. And here I begin:
This is a story they'll repeat
Forever, in Christian lands.
Chrétien of Troyes says so.
One Easter day, in springtime,
King Arthur was holding court
At Castle Cardigan.
Crowds of bold knights, courageous,
Strong, and proud, with noble
Ladies and girls, beautiful
Daughters of kings, made it
The most splendid sight in the world.
But before dismissing court
That day, the king declared
He wished to hunt the white stag,
Reviving that custom. And hearing
The king's words, my lord
Gawain was strongly displeased.
"Your majesty: you've little
To gain, hunting that beast.
We all know how it works;
We've always known. Whoever's
Able to kill a white stag
Wins the right to kiss
The prettiest girl in your court,
No matter who is offended.
Infinite evil may follow:

Hundreds of highborn young women
Are here, graceful, modest,
And not a one of them hasn't
Some bold and powerful knight
For a lover, who'd all argue—
Indifferent to right or wrong—
That the lady who drew his heart
Was loveliest, best, and most noble."
The king answered: "I'm well
Aware. But I won't change a word,
For once a king has spoken
No one's allowed to argue.
Early tomorrow morning
We'll all take our delight
Hunting that stag in the magical
Woods where wonders happen."
  So the hunt was set for the very
Next day, at dawn. And just
At sunrise the king rose
And made himself ready for riding
In the forest, wearing no armor
But only a short coat.
He had his knights awakened
And their horses equipped. When all
Were mounted, off they rode,
Taking their bows and arrows.
The queen rode behind them,
Along with one of her ladies,
Young, a king's daughter,
Mounted on a white palfrey.
And spurring his horse, a knight
Named Erec hurried after them,

A knight of the Round Table,
Who'd won great favor at court.
From the moment he first appeared—
So striking that nowhere on earth
Could you find a handsomer man—
No knight was better loved.
He was beautiful, noble, and brave
But barely twenty-five.
No one at only his age
Had proven himself so nobly.
What can I say in his praise?
Wrapped in an ermine cape,
He galloped down the road,
Riding a battle steed.
His undercoat was rich
Brocade from Constantinople.
His shoes were woven silk,
Beautifully cut and sewn,
And spurs of hammered gold
Were fixed and ready at his heels.
He carried no other arms
Than his sword; it was all he had brought.
He came alongside the queen
Just where the path had branched.
"My lady," he said, "if you like,
Wherever you ride I'll ride
Beside you. My only reason
For coming was to keep you company."
The queen thanked him, and said,
"Dear friend, believe me, no one's
Company could please me more;
I'd love to have you with me."

So saying, they rode straight on
And were soon into the forest.
Those who had gone ahead
Had already begun the chase.
The horns rang out, there were shouts,
Dogs went running after
The stag, leaping, barking.
Arrows flew through the air.
And the king, on a Spanish stallion,
Rode in front of them all.
Guinevere, trying to follow
The hounds, was in the woods
With Erec and her lady, a girl
Extremely beautiful and gracious.
But they'd gotten so far from the hunters
Chasing after the stag
That they couldn't hear a thing,
No horns or men or dogs.
So after trying as hard
As they could to locate some human
Sound, some trace of a hound
Yelping, they stopped beside
The road, in a clearing. And then,
Not long after, they saw
A knight approaching, mounted
And fully armored, his shield
Hung from his neck, his lance
In his hand. The queen had seen him
In the distance, and riding beside him,
To his right, a wellborn young woman,
And guiding them down the road,
Mounted on a well-worn nag,

A dwarf holding a leather
Whip knotted at the end.
And seeing so handsome a knight,
Queen Guinevere longed
To learn who he was, he
And the girl who rode beside him.
So she quickly ordered her royal
Maid to approach him. "My dear,"
Said the queen, "tell that knight
Riding toward us to come
To me, and bring that girl
With him." The maid turned
Her palfrey toward the knight,
Riding slowly, but the dwarf
Headed her off, waving
His whip in her face. "Stop,
Woman!" the creature cried,
As cruel as anyone alive,
"Why are you crossing toward us?
Come no further, I warn you!"
"Dwarf," she said, "let me pass.
I wish to speak to that knight,
Because my queen has sent me."
The dwarf, who was low-born, cruel,
And disgusting, blocked her path,
Crying, "You can't come here!
Go back where you came! You have
No right to address so good
A knight." The lady rode forward,
Intending to push past him,
Offended that a creature so tiny
Should block her way. Seeing her

Riding ahead, the dwarf
Raised his knotted whip,
Meaning to strike her full
In the face, and she threw up her arms,
And he struck a fierce blow
Across her uncovered skin,
Hitting so hard that the whole
Back of her hand turned
Blue. Like it or not,
The girl was forced to return,
Weeping as she went, tears
Flowing freely from her eyes
And rolling down her face.
What was the queen to do,
Seeing her maid so wounded?
Angry, and deeply upset,
She said, "Erec, my friend!
How it pains me, watching
My maid beaten by this dwarf.
This knight is a vulgar boor,
Allowing such a scoundrel
To beat this beautiful girl.
Erec, dear friend, go
To him, tell him wicked
Behavior must stop, tell him
To come to me, I wish
To know him, and the lady." Erec
Went at once, spurring
His horse directly toward
The knight. The malicious dwarf
Quickly barred the way.
"Fellow," he said, "stay back!

Where do you think you're going?
Back where you came from, I say!"
"Enough," said Erec, "you ugly
Dwarf, cruel and quarrelsome!
Out of my way!" "Stay there!"
"I'm coming." "No, you're not!"
Erec pushed forward, but the dwarf,
Vilest creature alive,
With a violent stroke of his whip
Slashed at Erec's neck.
The young knight's neck and face
Were deeply cut, every
Knotted strand leaving
Visible marks all over.
But Erec knew he couldn't
Strike the dwarf, as he wished to,
Seeing the other knight's fearsome
Weapons and, knowing his malice,
Sure the knight would kill him
If he struck the dwarf in his presence.
Courage doesn't mean madness,
And Erec was more than wise
Enough to know when to stop.
"My lady," he explained, "It gets worse
And worse. This wicked dwarf
Has cut up my face, yet I can't
Kill him, I can't touch him.
But no one would blame me, knowing
I have no weapons, no armor,
And this vile, outrageous fellow,
Does, and wouldn't, I think,
Take it lightly: he's haughty

Enough to kill me on the spot.
But let me promise you this:
If and when I can,
I'll either revenge myself
For these miserable wounds or be shamed
Forever. But I left my armor
And weapons at Cardigan,
This morning, and now they're far
Away, when I need them. If I went
To fetch them, I'd probably never
Find this fellow again,
Riding so quickly along.
So I've got to follow behind him,
No matter how far he goes,
Until I can buy or borrow
Weapons and armor. If I find
Someone to lend me what I need
Then, soon enough, this knight
Will find himself in combat.
And trust me, make no mistake:
Once we're fighting only one
Can win, him or me.
And I'll return, if I can,
Three days from now. You'll see me
At the palace, but whether sad
Or happy, I've no idea.
My lady, there's no more time:
I've got to follow that knight.
I'm going. May God bless you."
And the queen, too, commended
Him to God, with a thousand
Prayers to keep him from harm.

Then Erec left the queen,
Riding hard behind
The knight. And the queen stayed
In that forest where the king was hunting.
Once the stag was caught
The king was the first to join her,
For the stag having been taken
And killed, they could head home,
Carrying the dead deer,
And were soon at Cardigan
Again. They dined, and when all
The knights had feasted and were happy,
The king, according to custom
(For he had taken the stag),
Declared he had earned a kiss
And would take what tradition offered him.
Whispers went sweeping across
The court, everyone sure
That nothing but lances and swords
Would settle the coming quarrel,
Each of the knights too proud
To agree that any woman
Could match the one he worshiped:
This was a risky affair.
Believe me, Gawain was not
Happy when he heard what was happening,
And said to the king, "My lord,
You can see that all your knights
Are troubled. All they can talk of
Is this cursèd kiss. All of them
Say it will never happen
Without quarreling and combat."

And the wise king replied,
"What's your advice, my dear
Nephew, for preserving honor
And my realm? I shouldn't start up
Quarrels." The best barons
At court hurried to advise him.
King Ydier was the first
To speak his mind, and then
King Cadovalant, wise
As he was noble and brave.
Then Kay, and Girflet, and then
King Amaugin, and many
Many more of his knights
And barons gathered around him.
Discussion went on and on
Till finally the queen arrived
And told them the adventure she'd met with
Deep in the forest—how she'd seen
An armored knight, with a savage
Little dwarf, and the dwarf
Had struck her lady's maid
On the bare hand with a knotted
Whip and lashed out, even
Harder, at Erec's face.
And Erec, shamed but unarmed,
Had followed the knight, hunting
Revenge, saying he'd be back
In three days, were he able to return.
"My lord," said the queen to the king,
"Hear what I have to say:
If your knights will give their consent
Hold off your kiss for these

Three days and Erec's return."
None of the knights objected,
And the king himself agreed.
   Erec galloped along
Behind the armored knight
And the wicked dwarf with his whip,
Until they came to a great
Castle, strong and beautifully
Built. They rode right through
The gate. Inside, there were knights
And ladies rejoicing—and that castle
Was filled with beautiful women.
You could see people feeding
Molting falcons and hawks;
Others were fetching sparrow
Hawks and peregrines;
Elsewhere they were playing games
Of chance, some rolling dice,
Some playing backgammon or chess.
Out in front of the stables
Young men curried and rubbed down
Horses. Ladies primped
In their boudoirs. They'd seen the armored
Knight, whom they knew, coming,
Along with his dwarf and his woman,
And three by three they came out,
Glad to salute and greet him.
But Erec, who was simply a stranger,
They utterly ignored.
And Erec followed the knight
Straight across the courtyard,
Till he'd shut himself in a room.

Seeing him safely housed,
Erec could not have been happier.
Going a little farther,
He saw an elderly man
Of the lower nobility reclining
On the steps of a shabby house,
A good, gray-bearded, honorable
Man, fine-featured, courteous.
He was sitting all alone,
Obviously lost in thought.
He had the look of a sensible
Man, who'd offer a visitor
Shelter. Erec approached,
And the old knight hurried to meet him.
Before Erec could speak,
The old man bowed in greeting.
"Good lord," he said, "be welcome!
And be my guest, if you will:
My house is ready to receive you."
Erec answered, "My thanks.
I come seeking shelter
For the night, a bed and a roof."
  Erec dismounted, and the old man
Himself took in his horse,
Led it in by the bridle,
Knowing his household honored.
And then he summoned his wife,
And his daughter, wonderfully lovely;
They'd been busy, off in a workroom;
I've no idea what they made.
The lady came out, and her daughter
With her, wearing a delicate

White chemise, cut wide
And pleated, and over that
A tunic, also white,
But wearing nothing else.
The tunic was terribly old,
And her elbows poked clean through.
But wrapped in rags as she was,
The body inside was beautiful.
A truly wellborn girl
On whom Nature had lavished every
Blessing and grace she knew,
Until even Nature herself
Wondered a hundred times over
How, just this once,
She'd fashioned such a perfect
Thing, for no matter how hard
She tried to match the model
She never could make another.
So Nature herself was proof
That no one in the world had ever
Seen such loveliness before.
I tell you, Iseult the Blonde
Couldn't boast such shining, golden
Hair: there was no comparison.
Her forehead, her features shone
Brighter and whiter than the lily.
Her skin glowed so fair,
So fresh and roselike, that no one
But Nature could have created it,
Lighting up her face.
Her eyes sparkled so clear
They seemed like a pair of stars.

God Himself couldn't make
A more perfect mouth or nose.
How describe such beauty?
I can say this much: surely
She was meant to be seen, to be stared at,
For looking at her was like
Seeing yourself in a mirror.
  Down she'd come from that workroom,
But seeing their guest, a knight
Of whom she knew nothing, she stopped
And carefully drew herself back:
Uncertain just who he was,
She turned shy, and her face reddened.
And Erec, seeing such dazzling
Beauty, was overwhelmed.
The old man said to his daughter,
"My sweet good child, take
This horse and lead it straight
To the stable where my own are kept.
Make sure it lacks for nothing,
Unbuckle its saddle and bridle,
Set out oats and hay,
Curry and brush it well,
See it has all it needs."
The girl then took the horse,
Unlaced its armored breastplate,
Took off its saddle and bridle.
The beast was in very good hands:
She devoted herself to its care,
Covering its head with a halter
And a padded collar, curried
And combed it, tied on a feedbag

And filled it with plenty of hay
And oats, all clean and fresh.
And then she came back to her father,
Who said, "My dear daughter,
Now take this knight by the hand
And honor his presence in our house
By showing him up to his room."
The girl was courtesy
Itself, and never held back.
She led him off by the hand.
Her mother had gone up first
To see that the room was readied,
And covered over the bed
With embroidered quilts and blankets,
On which the three of them sat,
Erec, his host to one side,
His host's daughter on the other.
A hot, clear fire was burning.
The good old man had only
A single servant, no chamber-
Maid, no groom, no boy,
And this servant was in the kitchen,
Cooking meat and fowl
For dinner. She was wonderfully deft,
Able to quickly and carefully
Boil beef and roast
Fowl. And when the meal
Was ready, she brought them water
In a pair of basins, laid out
Cloths and napkins, bread
And wine, quickly and well.
They seated themselves at the table.

Whatever they wanted and needed
Was waiting ready to hand.
And when they all had dined
At their leisure, and risen from the table,
Erec inquired of his host,
Lord and master of the house:
"Tell me, good host," he said,
"Why your daughter, so good,
So beautiful a girl, wears
Such a torn and tattered dress?"
"My friend," the old man told him,
"Poverty injures many
Men, and I am one of them.
It hurts me, seeing my daughter
Dressed so poorly, but I've no
Way to make it better.
Most of my life has been spent
At war, and I've lost, or sold,
Or mortgaged all my land.
And still, she'd wear the finest
Clothes if I'd let her accept
The gifts they've tried to give her.
Even the lord of this castle
Would have dressed her in lovely clothes
And given her whatever she wanted,
For he's a count and she's
His niece. And any baron
In this land, no matter how rich
Or powerful, would be glad to have her
For his wife, whatever my terms.
But I want some grander match,
If God's grace provides it

And He will send us, here,
Some mighty king or count,
For could any emperor or king
On earth be shamed, taking
My beautiful daughter, so wonderfully
Lovely that no one's her equal?
Her beauty's magical, but her mind
And heart are worth still more.
God has never created
A creature so noble and good.
With her beside me, the rest
Of the world means less than a billiard
Ball: she's pleasure, she's joy,
She's solace, she's comfort, she's all
I own and all I treasure.
There's nothing on earth I love more."
Then having heard his host's
Story, Erec asked him
Why so many knights
And ladies had congregated
There in that castle, so that every
Miserable alley and every
House no matter how poor
Or small was filled with knights
And ladies and squires. And the good
Old man explained it like this:
"My friend, these are barons
From all the counties around,
Young and also old,
Come for a celebration
To be held at the castle tomorrow.
That's why our houses are packed.

That's why the streets will be seething,
Tomorrow, when everyone's here,
For a silver perch will be set
In front of them all, bearing
A splendid sparrow hawk,
Molted five or six times,
The best that's ever been seen.
And whoever would have this hawk
Must have a wise and beautiful
Woman totally unstained.
Any knight brave
Enough to risk his lady's
Good name, and her honor, is free
To lift that hawk from its perch
And carry it off, with everyone
Watching—at least, if no one
Dares object. We keep
This custom, and everyone comes
Each year to observe it." Erec
Replied, pressing him further:
"Good host, I've no wish to annoy you,
But tell me, if you know, that knight's
Name, with arms of blue
And gold, who rode past your door
Just now, a charming girl
Close at his side, and riding
Before them a humpbacked dwarf?"
And then the host replied,
"He'll take the hawk, that one,
And no one will dare oppose him.
No one will stand and object,
There'll be no fighting, no bloodshed.

He's already taken it twice
In a row, without protest.
If he gets it again, this year,
It's his forever more:
He'll have it every year,
Without any quarrel or battle."
Erec responded at once,
"I've no affection for this knight!
Indeed, if I'd weapons and armor
I'd challenge his claim to that hawk.
Good host, help me, please:
In the name of all that's noble,
And your own kindness, I beg you,
Tell me how I can find
What I need, old or new,
No matter how fine or ugly."
His host answered him openly,
"Be calm, young man, don't worry:
I've excellent weapons and armor,
I'll gladly lend what you need.
I've a triple-woven mail shirt,
Chosen one in a thousand,
Gleaming leg-armor beautifully
Made, light and handsome,
And a perfect, polished helmet,
And a dazzling brand-new sword.
A horse, a rapier, a lance—
I can lend you it all, and I will.
Don't say another word."
"Good sir, a thousand thanks!
But I need no better sword
Than the one I've got, nor any

Better horse: these
Will serve me perfectly well.
Lend me the rest, good sir,
And you'll grant my every wish.
Except for one thing more:
I've one more request to make,
And it's one for which I'll repay you,
Should God grant me victory."
His host answered in kind,
"Ask whatever you want
For your pleasure, whatever it is:
Anything I have is yours."
Then Erec said he wanted
To claim that hawk in his daughter's
Name, for no woman alive
Enjoyed a hundredth part
Of her beauty, and taking her with him
Would give him certain right
And reason to show that the hawk
Belonged to her alone.
And he added, "Good sir, let
Me tell you what manner of man
I am, my rank, my birth.
I'm the son of a powerful king:
My name among the Bretons
Is Erec, son of Lac.
I'm one of the knights of King Arthur,
At whose court I've spent three years.
I've no idea if my father's
Name or mine have ever
Reached your ears, but I promise you
This, on my solemn oath:

Lend me your weapons and armor,
Trust your daughter to me,
And tomorrow I'll fight for that hawk,
And if God gives me victory
I'll take your daughter to my country
And have her crowned as my queen,
Ruler of three cities."
"Ha! Is this all true?
Are you really Erec, Lac's son?"
"Good sir, at your service, in the flesh."
It was easy to see his host's
Happiness. "Of course we've heard
Of you, they talk of you often.
I love and respect you still more,
Knowing your courage, your strength.
How could I ever refuse you?
I give you my lovely daughter,
You may have her, body and soul."
He took his daughter's hand:
"Take her," he said. "She's yours."
Erec accepted with pleasure:
Now he had all he had wanted.
The entire household was happy,
The father as pleased as could be,
The mother weeping for joy,
And the girl herself, though silent,
Delighted by the wonderful luck
God had granted her: wise
And noble, she knew he'd be
A king and she his queen,
Honored and royal, wearing
A rich, majestic crown.

They sat up late, that night.
White sheets were put on the beds,
And down-soft quilts, and they finally
Stopped talking and all went happily
Off to sleep. But that night
Erec slept little. Next morning,
As dawn broke, he rose
And quickly got himself ready,
He and his host together.
And together they went to church
To pray and have a monk
Sing them a Mass to the Holy
Spirit, and they left an offering.
And having heard that Mass
Each of them bowed at the altar,
And then they returned to the house.
Erec was anxious for battle.
He asked for his armor, which was brought,
And the girl herself armed him,
Employing neither magic
Nor spells, but fastening with deer-hide
Thongs his leg armor, putting
The fine-meshed mail around him
And lacing it tightly in place.
With the burnished helmet on his head
He was armed from top to toe.
And at last, his sword strapped
To his belt, he called for his horse,
And as they led it in
He leapt on its back with a bound.
The girl brought in his shield
And his tempered, sharp-pointed lance.

She gave him the shield, which he took
And hung from his neck by its strap.
Then she put the lance in his hand;
He held it low on the handle,
Then said to his open-hearted
Host, "Good lord, if you please,
Let your daughter be ready!
I'll lead her, now, to that hawk,
As you and I have agreed."
Without the slightest delay
The good old man saddled
Up a bay-colored palfrey.
But I've nothing to say of its trappings:
There weren't any, on account of
The empty purse he'd acknowledged.
She had only saddle and bridle.
No cloak on her shoulders, her head
Bare, and with little time
For prayer, the girl mounted.
Erec couldn't wait to leave,
So he left, leading his host's
Daughter at his side, the girl's
Father and mother following
Along behind. Erec
Rode with his lance erect,
And the girl on his right. Everyone
Stared as they came, people
Both high and low, amazed
At the sight, questioning each other,
And trying to understand.
"What's this? Who's that knight?
He's bound to be brave, and fierce,

With that beautiful girl beside him.
He won't be wasting his time,
Claiming that someone so lovely
Is the loveliest one of all."
Some of them said, "By God,
He's going to get that hawk."
Some of them sang the girl's
Praises, and many exclaimed,
"Lord! Who could he be,
That knight with his beautiful lady?"
"Who knows? Who knows?" some said,
"But that helmet's a work of art,
And that mail shirt." "Just look at that shield."
"And the steel-tipped lance in his hand."
"He knows how to sit on a horse,
He looks like a wellborn knight."
"Oh, he's well built: look at
Those arms, those legs, those feet."
Every eye was on them,
But Erec never stopped
Till he stood in front of the hawk.
And then he drew to the side,
Awaiting the other knight.
  And there he was, coming
With his dwarf and his lady beside him.
He'd heard the news already:
Some knight who wanted the hawk
Had made an appearance, but he never
Dreamed the world contained
Anyone brave enough
Actually to stand and oppose him;
He was sure he could crush any challenge.

They all knew who he was
And crowded around to greet him.
A great press of knights
And squires pushed along
Behind him, and ladies running
After, and girls scampering.
He rode in front of them all,
He, and his woman, and his miniature
Man. He cantered up
To the hawk, bursting with pride.
But so many excited peasants
Had crowded around that he couldn't
Approach a bit closer
Than a long crossbow shot.
Then the count of that castle rode
His horse straight at the peasants,
Shaking a staff at their heads,
And the louts fell back. Then the knight
Rode up, his voice and manner
Calm, and addressed his lady:
  "My dear one! This wonderfully molted
Bird, this beautiful hawk,
Belongs to you by right,
Gracious and lovely as you are.
It is yours for as long as I live.
My sweet one, come forward, take
This bird from its silver perch."
The lady put out her hand,
But Erec quickly challenged her,
Indifferent to her knight's disdain:
"No, my dear," he said,
"Play with something else.

You have no right to this bird.
No matter who may not like it
You'll never own this hawk,
For someone else deserves it,
More beautiful still, and more noble."
The other knight glowered,
Which didn't bother Erec.
He called to his own lady:
"Come forward, my lovely," he said,
"And lift this bird from its perch,
For it's only right that you have it.
My beauty, come forward and take it!
For here and now I say
No woman alive can match you,
Any more than the moon
The sun, not for courage,
Loveliness, courtesy, or honor.
Let anyone dare deny it!"
The other knight was furious,
Hearing Erec so boldly
Challenge him and his lady.
"Fellow, who are you,
Presuming to contradict me?"
Erec answered him clearly:
"A knight from another land,
Come to hunt this hawk,
Knowing my lady deserves it
No matter what anyone thinks."
"You'd better run while you can:
Foolishness led you here.
Try to take this hawk
And you'll pay a terrible price."

"Really? What price did you have
In mind?" "I'll have that hawk
Or here and now we fight."
"That," said Erec, "is truly
Folly, mere empty words
For frightening children, not me.
I scarcely tremble at the thought."
"Then here and now I challenge
You to mortal combat."
"Let God decide," said Erec.
"I wanted nothing else."
So now you'll hear some fighting!

They cleared away a great space,
And the crowd pushed around it.
The knights measured their steps
Back, then spurred their horses
Forward, spearheads crashing,
Rushing so fiercely together
That their shields were battered and cracked,
Their lances smashed to bits,
Their very saddles destroyed.
They were forced to leap from the stirrups
Down to the ground, letting
Their horses run free in the fields.
Spears having done what they could,
They attacked each other on foot,
Drawing forth their swords
And slashing fearsome strokes,
Hacking such heavy blows

That their helmets rang and shattered.
They fought ferociously, cutting
Hard at each other's necks,
For this was no make-believe combat:
They smashed whatever they could,
Swords slicing, mail shirts
Crackling, iron red
With blood. On and on
They fought, so fierce, so savage
That resolve weakened, and their arms.
The two women were in tears:
The knights saw their ladies
Raising their hands to God,
Begging that victory go
To him who suffered for her.
  And the other one said to Erec:
"Knight! Let's both step back
And rest for just a moment:
Our blows have gotten too feeble.
We need to strike harder,
For it's getting close to dark.
It's shameful, we lose honor,
Letting this last so long.
Look at that lovely girl
Calling to Heaven on your
Account; how sweetly she prays;
And my lady, too. These steel
Blades must do their work
Better, and for them." And Erec
Answered, "You've spoken well."
They rested a little while.
Erec watched his beloved

Sweetly praying. And as soon
As he saw her, he felt his strength
Returning, his courage renewed.
The sight of her beauty, and the force
Of his love, doubled his resolve.
And he thought of the queen, and how
He had told her, there in the forest,
He would take revenge for the dwarf's
Insult, and he hadn't done it.
"Scoundrel!" he thought. "Why
This delay? I need to revenge
The vileness this knight allowed
His dwarf to commit, there
In that wood." His anger rose
Again, and he cried to his enemy:
"Knight! I call you back
To battle. We've taken quite
As long a rest as we need.
There's combat still to be fought."
The knight answered: "Agreed."
They threw themselves back into battle.
Both were trained swordsmen:
In the first assault if Erec
Had lowered his guard his enemy's
Sword would have pierced his skin.
Reaching around Erec's
Shield, he caught him across
The head, breaking part of
His helmet. The sword cut
Down to the white cap
Worn beneath, slicing
The shield halfway through,

Slashing off a chunk
Of mail shirt. Erec would have
Been badly hurt: he felt
The cold steel on his hip.
But God saved him, that time:
A little further in
And he'd have been split down the middle.
Erec wasn't worried:
Whatever he got, he'd give back.
A fierce swing of his sword
Across the other's shoulder
Fell so swift and sure
That the shield crumpled, and the mail shirt
Was worthless, and the sharp blade
Stabbed clear to the bone;
Rivers of red blood
Went running down to his waist.
Both were superb warriors:
They fought so equally neither
Could gain an inch on the other,
Could find no way to win.
Both their mail shirts were torn
And tattered, both shields so cut
And chopped you couldn't claim
Either had any protection
Left. They stood face to face,
Fighting, both of them bleeding
Freely, both of them weak.
He struck Erec, and Erec
Struck him; they'd been beaten so hard
On the helmet they both were stunned.
They swung at each other, without

Resistance. Then Erec landed
Three smashing blows, breaking
His enemy's helmet, slicing
His cap, cutting part
Of the skull away, but stopping
Short of the brain. His enemy
Tottered, and seeing him buckling
Erec pushed him, and he fell,
Stretched out, right hand down.
Then Erec seized him by the head,
Ripped away the rest
Of his helmet and unfastened the visor,
Uncovering his face. Remembering
How this knight's ugly dwarf
Had acted, back in the wood,
He would have cut off his head,
But the beaten man begged
For mercy. "Knight! You've won.
Have mercy! Don't kill me—please.
Now that I'm conquered, my death
Can bring you neither honor
Nor fame. If you killed me
My death would bring you disgrace.
Here is my sword: take it."
Erec would not take it.
But he said: "All right. You may live."
"Thank you, noble knight!
What wrong, what crime, could make you
Hate me and kill for that hate?
I've never seen you before,
As far as I know, or harmed you,
Or insulted or shamed you. Never."

Erec replied: "You have."
"What?" the other knight said.
"I don't remember your face.
But if I've done you mischief
I pledge you eternal faith."
Then Erec said: "Knight,
I rode in the forest beside
Queen Guinevere, when you let
Your haughty dwarf strike
My queen's maid. What a savage
Deed, striking a woman!
And then he did it to me.
You took me for some sort of serf:
What vile arrogance, to see
Such an outrage and, silent, allow
It to happen, and even take
Delight in watching that miserable
Midget injure the girl
And me. Despise you? Of course,
For what was done to us both.
Pledge yourself my prisoner,
And then, without delay,
Go directly to the queen:
You'll find her at Cardigan castle.
Ride there. You can reach that castle
Tonight, surely: it can't
Be more than twenty miles off.
You, your woman, and your dwarf
Must place yourselves at her
Command and do as she wishes.
And give her this message: tomorrow
I mean to return, happily,

Bringing a wellborn woman
So lovely, so noble, so wise,
That no one could find her equal.
You will tell her exactly that.
And now, tell me your name."
Willy-nilly, the knight
Answered: "My lord, I'm Ydier,
The son of Nudd. Yesterday
Morning I couldn't have imagined
Any knight could defeat me.
I've found my better, it's been proven:
An immensely powerful knight.
You have my promise, I swear
To do as you wish, at once,
And surrender myself to your queen.
But please don't hide your own name:
Tell me what to call you;
Who shall I say has sent me?
I'm almost ready to leave."
Erec replied: "I'll tell you
My name, there's nothing to hide.
I'm Erec. Now go to the queen
And say it was I who sent you."
"I'm going, you have my word.
My dwarf and my woman join me,
All of us wholly at
Her mercy. Rest assured.
And I'll give the queen news
Of you and of your lady."
Erec accepted his word.
Then everyone came to see
The account settled, the count

And his neighbors, ladies and barons.
Some were sad and some
Were happy: some pleased, some not.
But everyone there rejoiced
For the girl in the white dress,
The poor knight's daughter,
For her heart was noble and true.
Ydier's fate made some of them
Mournful, and one was his lady.
And Ydier could stay no longer;
His pledge obliged him to leave.
He mounted his horse. — But why
Bore you with all the details?
Leading his dwarf and his lady
He crossed both wood and plain,
Making his way straight
To Cardigan castle, and came there.
And just outside the hall
Were my lord Gawain, and Kay,
The king's steward, and many
Other knights, I suspect,
With them. Gawain and Kay
Were watching the new arrivals,
And Kay was the first to know them.
He said to Gawain: "My lord,
Unless I'm wrong, that knight
Coming along the road
Is the rude fellow the queen
Spoke of, who grossly insulted her.
I see three of them coming,
One knight, one dwarf, one lady."
"Quite so," Gawain agreed,

"I see a girl and a dwarf
Riding along with a knight,
And they're coming straight toward us.
He's armored, with all his weapons,
But his shield is badly broken.
It seems to me the queen
Will know him as soon as she sees him.
Go, steward, call her!"
Kay went at once
And found her in one of the rooms.
"My lady," he said, "remember
The dwarf who wounded your maid
And made you so angry?" "Indeed,
I remember him very well.
Steward: have you learned something?
Why are you asking such questions?"
"My lady," he said, "I've seen
A knight errant approaching,
Mounted on a gray horse
And armed, and unless my eyes
Deceive me, leading a young
Lady. And he has a dwarf
Carrying, I think, the knotted
Whip that struck Erec."
The queen rose at once,
Saying: "Quickly, steward,
Let's see if this is truly
The man, and if it is
I'll know him at once, believe me,
The moment I see him." Kay said:
"I'll show you. Come to the upper
Rooms, where all our friends

Are gathered. We saw him first,
While standing there; my lord
Gawain awaits you. Hurry,
My lady: we've lingered too long
Down here." And the queen, excited,
Hurried just as he'd said,
And came to the window where lord
Gawain was waiting, and stood there
Beside him, and knew the knight
At once. "My lord, it's him!
And something serious has happened;
He's been in battle. Has Erec
Taken revenge? Who knows
If Erec defeated him
Or was vanquished himself. That shield's
Been battered; his mail shirt's covered
With blood; there's more red
Than white." "Indeed," said Gawain.
"My lady, who could doubt
You've seen it exactly right?
His mail shirt's spattered with blood;
He's badly battered: whatever
Battles he's fought were hard ones.
That's all we can tell for sure:
He's fought fiercely and long.
We'll hear things said, now,
To make us angry or proud.
Either Erec has sent him
To us, his prisoner and yours,
Or else he's such a fool
He's come to boast how he conquered
Erec, or killed him. Nothing

Else is possible." Then the queen
Answered: "You're right. I agree."
"Indeed," said all the others.
Then Ydier reached the gate,
Bringing them his news.
And everyone hurried down
To hear him, all of Arthur's
Knights. At the royal mounting
Block, Ydier dismounted.
Gawain took the lady's
Hand and helped her descend.
And the dwarf, too, came down
From his horse. More than a hundred
Knights were watching. The three
Were brought to the king. And as soon
As Ydier saw the queen
He bowed almost to the ground,
First greeting her and then
The king and the other knights,
And saying: "My lady, a gentleman
Sent me here as your captive,
A brave, courageous knight,
He whom my dwarf struck
On the face with his whip. He has beaten
Me in combat, I am vanquished.
Lady, I bring you my dwarf
As your prisoner, all at your mercy:
Do with him however you wish."
The queen could not remain silent,
But requested news of Erec.
"Tell me, sir," said she,
"Do you know when Erec is coming?"

"Tomorrow, lady. And he'll bring
A woman lovelier than any
I've ever seen on earth."
Then having heard his message
The wise and noble queen
Declared, courteously: "My friend,
Coming here as my captive
Your prison will weigh on you lightly:
I mean you no harm. But God
Help you, tell me your name."
And he answered her: "Lady,
I'm Ydier, the son of Nudd."
Everyone knew it was true.
Then the queen rose, and bowed
Low in front of the king
And said: "Your Majesty has heard?
You've waited for Erec, that valiant
Knight, and it's good that you've waited.
I gave you good counsel, yesterday,
Good advice that you took.
This proves what good advice
Is worth." Said the king: "You speak
An ancient and honorable truth:
Wise men have ears to hear with.
We did well to accept your words.
But now, if you love me even
A little, you'll free this knight
From his prison, with only one
Condition—that he stay forever
In my house and at my court.
And if he won't, the worse
For him!" The king had barely

Spoken when the queen, in proper
Form, proclaimed her captive
Paroled, provided he stayed
At her husband's court. The knight
Made no plea for mercy
And promised to stay where he was;
Thereafter he remained a part
Of that court where he'd never been
Before. Boys came running
To take his weapons and armor.
And now it is time to talk
Of Erec, still there where they'd fought
Their battle. Not even Tristan's
Victory over fierce Morholt,
On Saint-Sampson Island, was welcomed,
I think, with such rejoicing.
From great and small, from fat
And thin, praise poured forth.
His knighthood was sung to the skies,
The whole place exclaiming:
"God, what a knight! The best!"
When Erec returned to his chambers
Their happy words went with him,
Their laughter, their joy, and even
The count of that place praised him,
Saying: "My lord, if you please,
It's only right and proper
That you take your lodging with me,
You, the son of King Lac.
It would honor my house and me
To have you under my roof:
I intend to make you my lord.

Good sir, I beg your goodwill,
Allow me to offer you shelter."
Erec answered: "I mean
No offense, but I can't abandon
My host, who has heaped me with honor,
Granted his daughter's hand.
What nobler gift could he give me,
So lovely, so precious, so rich?"
"To be sure, my lord," said the count.
"As good as she is beautiful,
Surpassingly lovely, and wise,
And born of the best blood:
Indeed, her mother's my sister.
It warms my heart, having you
Condescend to my niece.
But let me urge you, once
Again, to lodge with me."
"Enough," said Erec. "It's out
Of the question. I can't and won't."
Seeing he couldn't prevail,
The count declared: "As you please,
My lord. We'll say no more.
But my knights and I propose
To join you, tonight, to keep you
Company and help you rejoice."
Erec thanked him for that promise.
And then he rode to his lodgings,
The count still at his side,
And knights and ladies behind them,
Every man delighted.
As soon as he reached there, twenty
Servants or more came running,

Happy to take off his armor.
The whole house was filled
With joyous people. Erec
Seated himself, and everyone
Sat in a circle around him,
On benches and beds and cushions.
The count reclined nearby,
The beautiful girl between them,
Her face shining, feeding
A plover's wing to the hawk
For whom the battle had been fought.
What honor and joy she'd won
That day, what royal grandeur!
No happiness could have been greater,
Nor was she shy about showing it.
She hid none of her joy,
And everyone there could see it.
But all in that house were happy
For her, for all loved her.
Then Erec summoned her father
And spoke handsomely, beginning
As follows: "Good friend, good host,
Good knight, you've honored me
Immensely, but your reward
Will be grander still. Tomorrow
Your daughter will come with me
To King Arthur's court, and there
I intend to make her my wife.
If you could kindly wait here
A little longer, I'll send for you,
Bring you to the land where my father
Rules and I will rule

After him; it's far, far off.
There I will give you two
Castles, rich and strong.
You'll be lord of Roadan, built
In the days of Adam, and another
Nearby castle just as
Noble. Montreval
Is its name. My father has none
Better. And in less than three days
I'll send you gold and silver,
And furs of every sort,
And good silk cloth, so you
May be dressed as you should, and your wife,
Too, who is now my dear
Sweet lady. At the crack of dawn
Tomorrow I shall lead your daughter,
Clothed as you see her now,
To King Arthur's court, where I'll ask
The queen to give her the clothes
She deserves, of bright red silk."
Also seated there,
Next to the lovely lady
In white, was a brave and noble
Girl, courteous and wise,
The lady's cousin and the count's
Niece, and hearing it said
That Erec's lady was to go
To Guinevere's court wearing
Nothing more than a tunic
She said to the count: "My lord,
How shameful for you, as well
As for her, should this knight bring her

To the royal court, your own
Niece, dressed so miserably."
And the count declared: "Please,
Sweet niece of mine, give her
The very best of your own
Clothing, to wear to court."
But hearing these words, Erec
Replied: "Please say no more,
Good sir. Do understand:
I wish my lady clothed
Only in robes given
Her by the queen herself."
To which the other girl
Replied, declaring: "Ha!
Good sir, since you propose
To lead my cousin off,
Dressed in this shabby white tunic,
Let me make you another
Offer. Since you insist
She can have none of my clothes,
Let me give her one
Of my three palfreys, horses
No king or count possesses.
One's sorrel, one's gray, one's dappled.
And truly, of any hundred
Palfreys, none is better
Than the dappled: no bird flying
Through the air can go as fast.
In all his life he's never
Stumbled: a child could ride him.
He's utterly perfect for a girl—
Not stubborn or restless, he doesn't

Bite or kick, he's calm.
Only an unsettled mind
Could hunt a better one. Riding
Him is as free of discomfort,
As easy, as sailing a boat."
Erec replied: "My sweet
Friend, the choice is hers:
She can certainly have him, if she likes,
And I too will be pleased."
The girl immediately called
One of her servants, and said:
"Go, my friend, fetch
My dappled palfrey. Saddle him,
Bring him here at once."
Her order was obeyed, the horse
Saddled and bridled, beautifully
Harnessed, and her servant climbed
On the shaggy-maned steed's back.
And then the horse appeared.
And seeing so fine, so noble
An animal, Erec heaped it
With praise, commanding one
Of his grooms to lead it to the stable
And house it there, next
To the horse he rode himself.
And then the evening ended,
The happy guests left.
The count returned to his home,
Leaving Erec with his host,
But vowing to be back in the morning,
Ready to escort him when he went.
They slept long and peacefully.

As dawn lit up the sky,
Erec prepared to depart,
Ordering his horses saddled
And his lovely lady awakened,
Who was already dressed and ready.
His host rose, with his wife,
Nor was there a knight or lady
Not waiting with them, glad
To go forth with Erec and the beautiful
Girl. Everyone mounted.
Erec rode with the count
On one side, the girl on the other,
And she didn't forget the hawk,
Playing with it as she went.
But she carried no other treasure.
They rode in a happy procession.
And when it was time to leave them,
The count wanted to honor
Erec, sending some
Of those knights and ladies along,
But Erec quickly declined,
Saying he needed no one
And wanted no one except
His beautiful lady. And then
He said: "I commend you to God."
The count and his people lingered,
But at last he kissed Erec
And his niece, and piously blessed them.
Her father and mother kissed her
Too, over and over,
And the mother wept as she left,
And the girl wept, and her father.

Love is like that, and nature,
And affection for the child you raise:
Parents cry with passion,
And sadness, and the tender love
They feel for their child. But father
And mother knew quite well
Their daughter left them only
To go to greater things.
But their love made them weep
Because their daughter was leaving.
They wept for no other reason,
Fully aware that in
The end she'd rise to great honor.
And as they rode away
In different directions, they wept
Piteously and blessed one another.
Erec hurried from his host,
Wildly anxious not
To be late at Arthur's court,
Happy and proud of the wonderfully
Beautiful, wise, and noble
Woman his valor had won.
He couldn't keep himself
From staring, and the more he looked
The better he liked her. From time
To time he bent and kissed her,
Riding as close as he could,
Refreshed, renewed at the very
Sight—her golden hair,
Her laughing eyes and smooth
Brow, her nose, her mouth,
All sweet, all moving his heart.

She was lovely, from top to bottom:
Her chin, her white throat,
Her hips and breasts, her arms,
Her hands. But the girl was staring
Just as hard, as if
Competing with the knight, her eyes
Warm, her heart loyal.
You couldn't have paid them to stop
Looking, each at the other.
They were perfectly matched in manners
And grace, in beauty, of birth
And blood equally noble—
So much alike, indeed,
In education and nature,
That even striving to tell
The truth, no one, seeing them
Together, could pick the better
Or more beautiful—so perfectly suited,
Even their hearts beat as one.
The laws of marriage had never
Joined a lovelier pair.
 They rode on together until,
Exactly at noon, they arrived
At Cardigan Castle, where all
Awaited their coming. The noblest
Barons in the king's court
Were perched at windows, watching.
And Guinevere was there,
And even the king, and Kay,
And Perceval from Wales,
And Gawain after him,
And Tor, King Ares' son,

And Lucan, the king's butler,
And many more good knights.
They saw Erec coming
From far away, bringing
His lady, and recognized
Their knight the moment they spied him.
The queen began to smile,
And the whole court was joyful,
Happy to welcome him back,
For knights and ladies alike
Loved him. When he reached the palace
The king came to greet him,
And the queen followed her husband.
All blessed Erec in the name
Of Our Lord; all praised his lady's
Beauty, which the king honored,
His royal hand helping her
Down from her horse: Arthur
Was exceedingly happy, a courtier
To the core, and honored her
Again, leading her in
To his marbled hall. Erec
And the queen came after, hand
In hand, and he said to her,
"My lady, I bring you the woman
I love, dressed in the same
Poor garments she wore when her father
Gave her into my care.
Nothing's been changed. She's daughter
To a poor and noble knight.
Poverty lowers many
Men, but her father honors

His rank, though he owns but little.
And her mother's a gracious lady,
Sister to a noble count.
There's nothing to make me refuse
Her hand; you can see her beauty;
Her blood is as good as any.
Poverty's forced her to wear
This white tunic until
Its sleeves are frayed at the elbow.
But I could have brought her here
Dressed in splendid clothes,
Because a girl, her cousin,
Offered her silken robes
With ermine and other furs,
But I wouldn't allow it, I wanted
Her to appear to you
Just as she came to me.
My sweet lady, look:
Surely she needs, you can see
For yourself, some elegant dress."
And the queen at once replied,
"You've done exactly as you should.
She ought to be wearing one
Of my gowns, one of the best,
A new one, fresh and beautiful."
The queen promptly led her
To her dressing room and ordered
That there be brought, at once,
A new under-tunic
And a green and purple-furred
Cloak, fresh made for royal
Use. The servant went

And returned with the rich cloak
And a tunic, trimmed (even
Its sleeves) with white ermine,
And its cuffs and collar, without
Exaggeration, adorned
With costly bands of beaten
Gold, and precious stones
Possessing rare powers—
Gray, violet, green,
And brown, all mounted in gold.
A splendid tunic indeed.
But the cloak, I assure you, was worth
Every bit as much.
Both were so utterly fresh
And new that they lacked fasteners
To close them. The finely made
Cloak had a collar fashioned
Of thick sable fur,
And golden clasps weighing
More than an ounce apiece,
One side bearing a ruby
Clearer than a red garnet,
The other a tawny orange jacinth.
And these fittings, too, were covered
With the finest, whitest ermine
Anyone had ever seen.
The purple fur was elaborately
Worked with dozens of crosses
Of every shape and color,
Cinnabar, violet, azure
Blue, green, and yellow.
The queen directed that five

Lengths of gold and silken
Thread be brought for fasteners.
Her servants carried them in,
Rich and beautifully worked.
And the queen insisted the cloak
Be put in order at once,
Assigning the task to a past
Master of all such work.
And when it was done, that noble,
Deep-hearted lady embraced
The girl in the bare white tunic,
Saying these generous words:
"My dear girl, I wish you
To exchange that tunic of yours
For this one, worth a hundred
Silver marks, so much
Do I wish to honor you. And wear
This cloak over it: in time
I'll give you more." She could not
Refuse, but took it, and thanked
The queen. And then two maids
Led her to a secluded room,
Where they took off her old tunic
(Worth less than a straw)
And dressed her in the new, which she fastened
With a rich embroidered belt,
Ordering the old one given
To the poor, for the love of God.
And then she clasped on the cloak.
No one could think of ignoring her
Now; her clothing was brilliant,
Bright, and made her even more

Beautiful. The maids bound up
Her flowing yellow locks
With golden ribbon, but that glowing
Gold couldn't shine as bright
As her hair. And on her head
They set a circle of hammered
Gold, shaped and colored
Like flowers. They wanted her looking
So lovely that no one could find
A thing to improve, and they worked
Hard. One of them placed
Around her neck a double
Strand of inlaid gold,
Mounted with a topaz. She'd become
So lovely, and Nature had formed her
So well, that in my opinion
Nowhere on earth could you find
Her equal. Then she emerged
And came to the queen, who was filled
With joy, seeing the result,
For she loved the lady, so pleasing
Were her gracious ways, and her beauty.
Then leading her by the hand
They came before the king,
And seeing them there, the king
Immediately rose to greet them.
And all the many knights
In that room, when they entered—so many
I could not account for a tenth,
A twentieth, or a thirtieth part
Of them all—rose as well.
But I'll tell you the names of the noblest

Barons, the best in the world,
Seated at the Round Table.
As always, the first among all
Those knights was Gawain, and Erec,
Son of Lac, was second,
And Lancelot of the Lake was third,
And Gornemant of Gort
Fourth, the Handsome Coward
Fifth, the Bold Monster
Sixth, Meliant from Lis
Seventh, the Accursed Wiseman
Eighth, Dodinel the Savage
Ninth—and let Gandelin
Be tenth, because of his goodness.
But I'll list the rest with no numbers,
For ranking such men is hard.
Yvain the brave sat some distance
Away, opposite Yvain
The Bastard, and unsmiling Tristan
Sat next to Blioberis.
Next came Short-Armed Cardoc,
A truly cheerful knight,
And Caveron of Robdic,
And then King Quenedic's son,
And then Quintarus's page,
And Ydier of Gloomy Mountain,
Gaheret, and Kay of Estral,
Amaugain, and Galet the Bald,
Girflet, Do's son, and Taulus,
Never tired of fighting,
And Loholt, Arthur's son,
A truly wonderful knight,

And Sagremor, who followed
No orders: he can't be forgotten,
Nor Bedvere, master of horses,
And master of checkers and chess,
Nor Bravant, nor King Lot,
Or Galgetin of Wales.
 And when the beautiful stranger
Saw so many knights
Seated in a circle and staring
At her, she bowed her head
In perfectly natural discomfort;
Her face turned red. But shame,
Too, suited her, made her
More beautiful. And seeing her discomfort,
The king drew her toward him,
Gently taking her hand
And seating her and the queen,
She to his right, the queen
To his left. Then Guinevere said,
" My lord, may I speak my mind?
A man who by force of arms
Can win so lovely a lady
In a foreign land, must be welcome
At your court. We were right to wait
For Erec, for now you can kiss
The loveliest woman here—
And no one, I think, will take
Offense, or term me untruthful,
If I call her the loveliest here
Among us, and in all the world."
 And the king answered, "You've told
The truth. And if no one disputes me,

The magic white stag's reward
Is hers." Then he asked his knights,
"How say you, gentlemen? Agreed?
It seems to me, without doubt,
That, face and body together,
This is the noblest, most beautiful
Woman from here to where
The earth touches the sky.
The magic stag's reward
Has got to be hers. Gentlemen:
Again, what do you think?
Has anyone any objection?
And if someone has a challenge
Let him speak his mind
Now. The king is never
Allowed to lie or encourage
Deceit or untruth or disorder:
Maintaining virtue and justice
Is the task of a loyal ruler,
Upholding the law, and truth,
And faith, and honest dealing.
Nothing could make me commit
Disloyal, dishonest acts
Against the strongest or weakest
Of men. No one should need
To accuse me. But neither do I wish
The customs and manners of my fathers
To fall by the way, just
As I never wish to abuse you
By making new laws, creating
Customs unknown to my fathers.
The laws my father, Pendragon,

Your king, your emperor, enforced,
Shall remain the living law
For you and for me. So tell me
Exactly what you think:
Does anyone disagree?
Is this, or isn't it, the loveliest
Woman at my court, entitled
To the white stag's kiss? I wish
To hear you; let the truth prevail!"
Then all of them cried as one:
"By God and the Holy Cross
You're right to call her the loveliest.
The sun has never shone
On any woman more beautiful.
Kiss her, here and now:
No one disagrees."
And seeing that all agreed
The king waited no longer.
Turning to the girl, he took her
In his arms. And the girl was too wise
Not to be pleased at this kiss,
Which only a peasant could resent.
The king kissed her as a courtier
Should, while his barons watched,
Then told her, "My sweet, I give you
My love sanely, as a gentleman
Should. I mean you no harm,
But love you from the bottom of my heart."
The king had restored the white stag's
Place in the customs of his court.
And here I finish Part One.

After the king's kiss
Had been given according to custom,
Erec, a noble and courteous
Knight, fulfilled—as honor
Required—the promises made
To his poverty-stricken host.
Keeping his word to the letter,
He promptly sent him five
Fat, well-rested horses,
Loaded with clothes and with cloth,
With buckram and other tight-woven
Stuff, and bars of silver
And gold, and squirrel fur,
And sable, and oriental
Silk. And once the mules
Had been heaped with everything a sensible
Man might require, ten knights
And ten household servants
And their helpers went with the animals,
Ordered to greet Erec's
Host, and also his wife,
With all the respect and honor
Erec's own heart could express,
And then to convey horses
And gold and silver and coins,
All the richness borne
In boxes on the horses' broad backs,
And then to escort the high lord
Of Outer Wales to his realm,
He and his wife together,

With all the honor due them.
Erec had promised two castles,
On the best sites, easiest
To defend, and most beautifully built
Of any castles on earth.
One was Montreval,
And the other was Roadan.
Once in that kingdom where his father
Ruled, Erec's men
Were instructed to be sure the castles
Were delivered, with all their rights
And rents, exactly as promised.
And those knights, and servants, and servants
Of servants, obeyed his orders:
Mules, and gold and silver,
And clothes, and coins, all
In immense profusion, were carried
To Erec's host and without
The slightest delay were handed
Over that very same day.
And showing the host the highest
Honor they knew, they led him
To his realm, a three-day journey.
King Lac had no objections
To his beloved son's arrangements,
And the castles and armored towers
Were delivered and their owner much honored,
With his title free and clear,
Guaranteed by the king,
And knights and merchants sworn
To observe and uphold their new lord's
Rights in every respect.

And when all of this had been done
Erec's men turned around
And headed home to their master.
He gave them a warm welcome,
Requesting news of his host
And his wife, and word of his father
The king. They gave him good tidings.
   And soon, the time fixed
For the wedding approached. Waiting
Had been hard for Erec; he couldn't
Wait much longer. He came
To the king, asking permission
To be married at court, without
Delay, and the king smiled
And gave him the consent he wanted,
And sent for all the counts
And dukes all over his kingdom
Who held their lands from his hand,
None of them bold enough
To refuse Arthur's invitation.
None of them keeping Pentecost
At home, they hurried to come
As their king had commanded them. Now listen,
And I'll tell you their noble names,
These kings and counts and dukes:
Count Branleigh of Gloucester was there,
With many richly armored
Men and a hundred horses.
And Menagorman came next,
Lord of Eglimon,
And also the lord of the Mountain-
Top, with many well-equipped

Men, and the count of Travain,
Together with a full five hundred.
And then came the count of Goodgrain
With at least as many more.
And along with all of these
Came Melwas, a powerful baron,
Lord of the Island of Glass,
Where no one ever hears thunder
Or sees lightning or storms,
Or any toads or snakes,
And it's never too cold or too warm.
And Grellemeuf of Finstere,
With twenty companions, and also
His brother, Guingemars,
Lord of Avalon Island
And said to be the lover
Of Morgana le Fay, a claim
History has proven true.
And David of Tintagel came,
Who never knew sadness or sorrow.
There were counts and dukes all over,
But even more kings: Garras,
The proud ruler of Cork,
With a full five hundred knights
All wearing tunics and cloaks
And breeches of taffeta silk.
Aguiflest, king
Of Scotland, rode a stallion
Of Cappadocian blood,
Accompanied by his sons, Cadret
And Cuoi, two powerful knights.
King Ban of Ganret came

With a crowd of beardless boys,
Faces smooth as a baby's,
Youngsters who served him at home,
Two hundred or more of the happiest,
Most cheerful pages on earth,
And each and every one of them
With a hawk or falcon on his wrist,
A merlin or sparrow hawk,
Molted birds, and goshawks.
The old king of Orcel,
Quirion, brought no youngsters,
But a troop of two hundred, not one of them
Under the age of a hundred,
Their heads grizzled and bald,
Their beards down to their belts,
From having lived so long.
They all were dear to King Arthur.
Bilis, lord of dwarves,
King of Antipodes,
And Bliant's cousin, was there,
A dwarf himself—indeed,
The smallest dwarf of all,
Just as his cousin Bliant
(By half a foot or more)
Was the tallest of Arthur's knights.
And to prove his power, and his wealth,
Bilis came with two dwarfish
Kings who ruled by his will,
Gribolo and Glodoalan.
Everyone marveled at these miniature
Men, but offered each of them
Honor and respect when they came

To court, arriving as kings
Of high and noble birth,
Surrounded by courtiers and servants.
At the sight of such an assembly
Of barons and counts and kings,
King Arthur's heart rejoiced.
And then, to heap his pleasure
Higher, he ordered baths
For a hundred pages, and made them
Knights, gave each rich robes
In many colors, of fur
And Egyptian silk, chosen
As each of them wished, and weapons
And armor, and a swift-footed horse
Worth at least a hundred
Pounds.
  Then Erec married
And was forced to reveal his wife's
True name, for a woman without
A Christian name cannot
Be married. No one had known
Her name, till now; they finally
Learned she'd been baptized Enide.
Canterbury's archbishop,
Who'd come to court himself,
Had performed the solemn rite.
And also assembled at Arthur's
Court was every musician
In all of England who could play
Or sing notes worth hearing.
They filled the palace with their pleasure.
Men were performing everywhere—

Some jumped, some tumbled, some sang,
Worked magic tricks, or whistled,
Some played the flute, the oboe
And the harp, and some the cello.
Circles of girls were dancing,
Everyone bursting with joy.
Nothing had been neglected
That could make men happy and fill
Their hearts with joy, that wedding
Day. Drums were beating,
And flutes and trumpets playing,
Oboes and clarinets.
How can I tell it all?
No inner doors, no gates
Were locked, people came
And went freely, all day:
No poor, no rich were kept
Away. King Arthur held back
Nothing: at the king's command
His cooks and bakers, and the stewards
Of his wine, provided meat
And drink and bread for everyone,
And as much as they liked. Anything
Anyone asked for was given,
And freely, no matter who
Or what, and all were well pleased.
   The palace rang with joy—
But enough of that: let me
Tell you the pleasure, the joy,
Experienced in bedroom and bed.
When the bridal night arrived
A bishop and archbishop led them

To their room. For this meeting
No one stole Iseult
Away or put Brangene
In her place! The queen herself
Prepared the bride for bed,
For love of both bride and groom.
No hunted stag, panting
With heat, thirsts for a fountain—
No starving sparrow hawk,
Hearing its name, comes flying
Eagerly back—more
Than these two hungered to hold
Each other. And they made up,
That night, for all their waiting.
The moment they were left alone
Every part of their bodies
Received its due. The eyes
(Which open love's way, carrying
Words to the heart) went back
To watching, and liked what they saw.
And once the words had arrived
They knew the even greater
Sweetness of kisses, and both
Relished the taste, drank
With all their heart, till it hurt
To remain apart. The game
Began with kisses. And love
So plainly shared prepared
The girl, gave her courage,
So nothing made her afraid,
She endured it all, no matter
What. And no longer a girl,

Rose the next morning a woman.
And each of the minstrels was happy,
Too, paid so wonderfully
Well their debts disappeared.
They were given handsome gifts,
Robes of rabbit fur,
Of squirrel and ermine, and violet
Silk, and brilliant red.
Whatever they wanted, horses,
Money, all received
Their heart's desire. The joy
Of that wedding feast lasted
Fifteen days, and more,
In glory and high magnificence,
Arthur affirming his lordship
And also honoring Erec
By keeping every one
Of his barons at court for a fortnight.
And when the third week came
They agreed to stage a tournament,
Later; my lord Gawain
Would wear the colors of one side,
And Melis and Meliadox
Would wear the colors of the other,
One of them standing for York,
The other for Edinburgh.
And then the court went home.
Pentecost came and was gone,
And after a month they convened
Their tournament out on a field
Near Edinburgh. Blue
And white and violet banners

Flew, and ladies' sleeves
And veils, all gifts of love.
And lances were everywhere,
Lances colored red
And blue, in gold and silver,
Wound and painted, striped
And spotted, bright and shining.
A host of helmets were laced,
That day, in iron and steel,
Green, yellow, red,
Gleaming in the sun against
The coats of arms, with a forest
Of silver mail shirts, swords
Belted on the left, shields
Fresh and new, painted
Blue and burning red,
With buckles of silver and gold,
And horses white and black,
Brown and bay, decked
With tassels, galloping back
And forth. Weapons and armor
Covered the field. And the knights
Were ready. The noise was tremendous,
Metal crashing on metal:
Lances shattered, shields
Cracked, mail shirts split.
Saddles were emptied, as knights
Went tumbling. Horses sweated
And foamed. And knights unsheathed
Their clanging swords, fighting
Over fallen bodies.
Some were captured, held

In parole; some ran into battle.
Riding a white charger,
Erec led the way,
All alone, seeking
His opponent, Orgueilleux de la Lande,
Mounted on an Irish horse
And riding fast and hard.
Erec struck so fiercely
At his shield, high on the chest,
That he drove him down to the ground.
And Orgueilleux left the field.
Wearing blue silk, Randuraz,
Son of Tergalo's widow,
Came riding at him, a famous,
Worthy knight. They attacked
Each other, hacking hard
At the shields hung from their necks.
A heavy blow from Erec's
Lance rolled him in the dirt.
Then Erec spun around,
Facing the king of Red City,
A valiant, courageous knight.
Clutching knotted reins,
Holding their shields by the straps,
They both wore fine armor
And rode good, rapid horses.
Striking hard, fierce,
At their fresh, new shields, each of them
Broke his lance. No one
Had ever seen such blows.
Shields and weapons, horses
And all, they came hurling together,

And neither reins nor straps
Nor saddle could keep the king
On his horse. He fell to the earth,
Still in his saddle, the reins
In his hands, everything falling
With him, sword and shield
And lance still at the ready.
And everyone watching that battle
Gaped, astonished, swearing
The price for fighting such
A knight was much too high.
But Erec wasn't hunting
Horses or knights, he wanted
Nothing but good fighting
That would show his spirit and strength.
All his opponents trembled,
And those who fought at his side
Felt their courage soaring.
He took captives, and horses,
But only to beat down his foes.
But let me tell you of Gawain,
Who conducted himself to perfection.
He defeated Guincel, first,
And then Gaudin of the Mountain.
He captured knights and horses:
Oh Lord Gawain did well.
Girflet, Do's son, and Yvain,
And Sagremor, who obeyed
No orders, fought so hard
They drove their opponents back
To the gates, and captured many.
And there in front of the castle

The battle began again,
Those inside fighting those outside.
And there Sagremor
Was beaten, a very great knight,
Captured and made a prisoner.
But Erec freed him. He began
By shattering his lance, smashing
An opponent full in the chest
And driving him off his saddle.
Then out came his sword, and he swung it,
Battering in their helmets.
And they fell back, allowing him
Through, even the strongest
Afraid. And he hit them so hard
That he drove them back in the castle
And Sagremor made his escape.
Then vespers rang out, and the fighting
Stopped. Erec's success
Had been greater than anyone there.
But the second day he did
Still better, captured so many
Knights, dashed so many
From their saddles that only those
Who saw it could ever believe it.
Every knight on either
Side declared him the victor:
His lance and his shield had triumphed.
Now Erec had grown so famous
That his name was in every mouth:
No man had been thought so handsome
Since Absalom walked the earth,
No man since Solomon so wise

In his words—fierce as a lion,
More open-handed than any
Lord since Alexander.
But once the tournament ended
Erec sought out the king,
Seeking permission to leave
The court and return to his home,
But first, as a courteous, noble
Knight, he thanked the king
For all the honors he'd received,
Which pleased him immensely. And only
Then did he explain
That he wished to leave for home,
Taking his new wife with him.
The king could hardly refuse,
Though he'd rather Erec stayed
Than went. So he gave him leave
But asked for a speedy return,
For of all the barons at court
Only one, his dear,
Incomparable nephew, Gawain,
Was Erec's rival in courage
And strength. Permission in hand,
Erec ordered his wife
To be ready. And the king sent
An escort of sixty mounted
Knights, wearing furs
And silks. Erec refused
To linger, leaving as soon
As he could, bidding the queen
A courtly farewell and commending
The knights of the court to God.

The sun had just risen when he rode
Away from the royal palace.
With everyone watching, he mounted
His horse; his wife, about
To leave her country, mounted
Hers. Then everyone mounted,
A hundred and forty men,
Knights and their squires. And then
For four whole days they journeyed,
Through forests and plains, up mountains
And hills, down slopes and rocky
Ground, and came, on the fifth day,
To Carnant, King Lac's home
And a wonderfully pleasant place,
A castle so beautifully set
That no one could imagine a better,
Surrounded by forests and prairies,
Vineyards and well-plowed fields,
Dotted with rivers and orchards,
Filled with knights and their ladies,
Brave, laughing young men,
Noble, learned scholars
Who spent their money well,
Beautiful, wellborn girls,
And wealthy merchants and traders.
And before he came to the castle
Erec dispatched a pair
Of messengers, informing the king
Of his coming. And as soon as he heard
This news, the king commanded
The entire court to mount
Their horses, men and women

Alike, and bells to be rung,
And all the streets hung
With silken cloths and banners,
Celebrating his son's
Return. Then the king mounted;
Eighty noble priests,
Honorable men in fur-trimmed,
Costly cloaks, rode with him,
And a full five hundred knights
On horses of every color,
And so many merchants and ladies
That no one could possibly count them.
Their horses ran so fast
That soon the king could see
His son, and his son saw him.
Leaving their horses, they walked
Into each other's arms.
And so they stood for a moment,
Neither willing to move,
Hugging and kissing each other.
The king had never been happier.
But then he stopped and turned,
Looking at his son's new wife,
And his happiness suddenly doubled.
He threw his arms around them,
Kissing, embracing them both,
Not certain who made him happiest.
And then they rode to the castle.
Every bell in every
Church rang out with Erec's
Return; the crowded streets
Were strewn with rushes and herbs,

And the walls draped with silk
And satin sheets, with cloth
Banners and tapestries. The king's
People filled the streets,
Welcomed the young prince,
Joy in all their hearts,
Young and old alike
Wild with delight. And first
They heard a mass sung,
And were welcomed at church by a solemn,
Pious procession. Erec
Knelt at the altar, prayed
On his knees in front of the Holy
Cross, and gave a gift
Of sixty silver bars,
Soon put to good use, and a gold
Crucifix Constantine
Had worn, containing a piece
Of the One True Cross on which
Our Lord suffered and died
For us, to free our souls
From eternal prison, snared
By Adam's sin, whispered
In his ear by the Evil One—
A priceless, ancient cross,
Studded with precious stones
Of great and wonderful power,
A giant ruby in the middle
And another at each end,
Beautifully set in gold.
No one has seen its equal.
At night each of those gems

Glittered as bright as the sun
At noon, shining in the sky—
Such a flood of light that the dark
Church needed no candles,
No chandeliers.
                    Two
Of the king's barons led
Enide to Our Lady's altar,
Where she most devoutly prayed
To Jesus and the Virgin Mary
That during her life, and her husband's,
They might be given an heir.
And then, as an offering, she gave
A wonderfully woven green
Silk cloth and a priestly cloak,
Covered with filigreed gold,
Made with all her skill
And care by Morgana le Fay
At her home in the Valley of Danger.
The silk was from Spain—and surely
Morgana had never made
The cloak for use in church,
But let one of her lovers
Have it because it was richly
Elegant. Guinevere,
Mighty King Arthur's wife,
Had deceived the Emperor Gassa
And gotten it, and had it used
To celebrate Mass in her chapel,
Because it was lovely. And when
Enide had left her, the queen
Had made it a gift for Erec's

Wife. It was said to be worth
A hundred ounces of silver.
And having made her offering,
Enide drew back a bit,
Silently signaling with her hand,
As only wellborn ladies
Can do. And then they went
Straight from the church to the palace,
And the celebration began.
Knights and burghers brought
Their presents to Erec: a gentle
Horse from Norway, for his wife;
A cup of hammered gold;
A young hawk; a grayhound,
And other dogs for hunting
Hares; a sharp-eyed falcon;
A Spanish battle stallion;
A sword; a painted banner;
A spear; a helmet. No king
Returning home was ever
Greeted with greater pleasure,
Welcomed with warmer joy.
Everyone wanted to serve him.
But his people's delight at lady
Enide was even wilder,
In part for her stunning beauty,
Still more for her gracious ways.
They sat her on a silken cushion
From far-off Thessaly,
And wellborn ladies crowded
Around her, there in that palace
Room. Just as a sparkling

Gem outshines a shard
Of flint, and the rose a dried-up
Poppy, so she outshone
Them all: nowhere in the world
Could anyone hope to find
A girl or a woman to match her—
Her breeding so clearly noble,
Her words so wise and cheerful,
Her manner so winning, so full
Of charm, that the sharpest critical
Eye would never see her
Foolish, or wicked, or mean.
She'd let herself be so
Well taught that she'd learned whatever
Women need to know,
And was open-handed and always
Alert. Her generosity
Was so delightful that kindness
To her was its own reward.
No one told tales of Enide,
For no one had tales to tell.
No woman in the kingdom, or beyond,
Carried herself so correctly.
  But Erec loved her with such
True love that, now, the God
Of War bored him. He left off
Attendance at tournaments;
All he wanted was his wife,
Who'd become both lover and friend.
Every waking moment
Went into hugging and kissing,
He needed nothing else.

Among themselves, his comrades
In arms lamented a love
So all-consuming; it pained them.
It was often afternoon
Before he rose from his bed
And joined them. Their pain was his pleasure.
But even lingering at her side
He remained attentive to their needs,
Never failing in his gifts
Of weapons, and garments, and gold.
And he sent his knights wherever
Tourneys were taking place,
With rich equipment and clothes.
He gave them sturdy horses,
Fit for traveling and combat,
And never cared about cost.
Still all his barons complained
Of how it pained them, and the shame,
For such a valiant knight
To have lost his interest in fighting.
Everyone blamed him, squires
And knights alike, until
Even Enide heard them
Saying her husband was now
Too lazy for chivalry and had thrown up
His knighthood; he led a new life.
These words weighed on her heart,
But she could not let him know,
For surely her husband would take it
Badly, were she to say
Such things. So she held her peace
Until, one day, as they lay

In bed, where they'd taken great pleasure,
Wrapped in each other's arms,
Their lips together, lovers
Sharing and delighting in love.
Erec slept; she did not,
Remembering words she'd heard
Spoken, up and down
The land, about her lord.
And the memory made her weep
In spite of herself. She could
Not stop. Indeed, those words
So weighed on her mind that, as luck
Would have it, her lips murmured
A few, intending no harm
And certainly not what happened.
She began to study her husband
From top to bottom, seeing him
Handsome of face and of body,
And suddenly wept such a flood
Of tears that some of them fell
Hot on his chest. "Oh Lord,"
She sobbed, "how hard it all is!
Was this why I left my home?
Let the earth open and swallow
Me down, for the best of knights,
The strongest, most loyal, the fiercest
In battle, courteous as no king
Could have been, and no count, has turned
His back on chivalry, and all
On account of me. Clearly,
His shame is completely my fault,
Though I'd never, never have wished it."

And then she said, "Beloved,
How you've been wronged!" That was all
She said. But his sleep was shallow,
Even as he slept he heard her.
Her words woke him, and he stared,
Astonished, seeing her tears
Flowing so fast. So he said:
"My love, my dear, my sweet,
Tell me what's caused these tears.
What's made you so angry? So sad?
I need to know, my beloved.
So tell me, my sweet, tell me,
Don't keep such sorrow secret.
Why did you say I'd been wronged?
I'm sure I heard you: you spoke
Of me—of no one else."
Then Enide was terribly flustered,
Deeply moved, and afraid.
"My lord," she said, "I don't
Understand a word you've said."
"My lady, why bother trying
To conceal it? You can't, I assure you.
You were weeping, I saw your tears,
And something caused them. I know it,
I heard you speaking through
Those tears, I heard what you said."
"But oh, my lord, you heard
Nothing, you only dreamt it."
"Now you're feeding me lies.
I know you're lying, I can hear it,
And you'll be terribly sorry,
Later, unless you admit it."

"My lord, because you oblige me
To speak, I'll tell the truth,
I'll hold back nothing, now.
But I'm much afraid it will hurt you.
Everyone—blonde, brunet,
And redhead—declares you've damaged
Your name by laying down
Your arms. Your reputation,
Your name, have tumbled to the ground.
Last year, all year, they all
Were saying no one knew
A better knight, or a braver;
No one alive was your equal.
Now you're a joke: young
And old, short and tall,
Call you a coward, a traitor.
Was it possible not to be pained,
Hearing my lord despised?
Their words pressed on my heart—
And all the more because
They laid the blame on me:
That was deeply painful,
Everyone saying I
Was the only cause, I
Had taken you captive, I
Had stolen your strength away
And left you thinking of nothing
But me. Consider, now,
How best to efface this slander
And restore your good name, for I've heard
Terrible things said
And never dared to tell you.

Often, remembering those words,
I could barely keep from crying.
But suddenly, just now, the pain
Was so great I couldn't contain it,
And I said that you'd been wronged."
"Lady," he said, "you were right,
And the things they said were true.
Quickly, prepare yourself
For a journey. Rise and put on
The most beautiful dress you own,
And have your saddle put
On your very best palfrey." Enide
Was overwhelmed with fear.
She rose, slow and sobered;
Left alone, her head
Whirled as she thought of her folly:
The ground's a better bed
When it isn't deep-plowed.
"What a fool
I am! Life was too good,
I had whatever I wanted.
Ah me! What made me so bold
That I spoke such insane words?
My God! Could my husband be too much
In love? Yes. He is.
So now he'll send me away!
But not seeing my lord,
Who loved me better than anyone
Else in the world, will be
The worst pain of all.
The best man ever
Born was so caught up

With me that he cared for no one
Else. Nothing was missing—
A happiness more than complete—
Until pride welled up and pushed me,
And I said such intemperate things.
My pride's become my punishment,
One I deserve. Suffering
Allows you to understand pleasure."
While she lamented, the lady
Dressed in her loveliest gown,
But nothing could please her, now,
Everything hurt her heart.
She sent one of her servants
To summon a young squire
And ordered him to saddle
Her sleek dappled palfrey:
Neither king nor count had a better one.
Without the slightest delay
The squire did as she had
Ordered, and the horse was saddled.
And Erec summoned another
Squire, ordering his arms
And armor brought. Ascending,
Then, to a palace room,
He ordered a Limoges cloth
Spread on the ground in front of him,
Then called the squire and commanded
Weapons and armor brought up
And placed there on that cloth.
And then he seated himself
As well on the cloth, directly
Upon the painted image

Of a leopard, and prepared to have
His body clothed in war gear.
First they laced gleaming
Armor over his legs,
Then put on a mail shirt so expensively
Made, so beautifully hammered,
That link by link it was utterly
Seamless, with not enough
Room to insert even
A needle, woven of intricately
Latticed silver and thus
Unable ever to rust,
So perfectly shaped and fitted,
Inside and out, let me
Assure you, that no one wearing
This shirt would feel more weary
Weight than a man comfortably
Draped in a garment of silk.
All his knights and squires
Were astonished, seeing him armored,
But no one dared ask questions.
The mail shirt in place, they fastened
On a circular helmet,
Gold studded with jewels
Shining brighter than mirrors.
He took up his sword and scabbard,
And ordered a saddle put
On his bay Gascony horse.
Then he called a servant and said,
"Fellow, quick, run
To the room next to the tower
Where you'll find my wife. Hurry,

Tell her I've waited too long;
She's had enough time to get dressed.
Tell her to come and mount
Her horse. I'm waiting." He ran
And found her all dressed, but pale
And weeping. He delivered his message
At once: "My lady, why
Are you lingering here? My lord
Is outside, waiting, wearing
His armor and ready to ride.
He says he could have been gone
Long since, had you been ready,
Too." Enide was stunned:
What might Erec be planning?
Still, she proceeded wisely,
Coming quickly to where
He stood, waiting, and acting
As happy as she possibly could.
King Lac came hurrying behind her,
And knights, too, were milling
About, old and young,
Wondering, asking each other
Who would go with their lord.
They offered themselves, humbly,
But he swore in front of them all
That no one would be his companion,
Only his wife, if she wished.
This meant he would ride alone.
King Lac addressed him, sadly:
"My son, what are you doing?
You need to tell me, in plain
Words, hiding nothing

From your father. Where are you going,
Completely alone, not a knight
Or a squire with you, in spite
Of all my pleas? If you plan
Some solitary combat,
Man to man, still
You ought to bring along
A troop of your knights, as much
For company as for protection:
A king's son can't ride
Alone. My son, take horses
With you, and at least some
Of your knights—thirty, or forty,
Or more, and silver and gold,
And whatever else a gentleman
Needs." Then Erec answered,
Telling his father why
He was making this journey. "My lord,"
He said, "I have no choice;
No other horse goes with me;
Silver and gold are pointless
Now, and squires and servants;
Except for my wife, I need
No one with me. But let me
Beg you, should I happen to die,
And she return, that you love
And cherish her, on account
Of my love and because I ask it,
And give her half your kingdom,
And let it be hers for the rest
Of her life, without dispute."
The king listened with care,

And said, "My son, she
Shall have it. But how it pains me,
Seeing you leave alone
Like this. It's not what I want."
"My lord, I have no choice.
I'm going. God protect you.
But don't forget my knights,
Give them horses and weapons
And everything knights require."
The king couldn't keep from weeping,
Seeing his son depart.
The entire court shed tears
With him, ladies and knights
So afflicted with passionate sorrow
On the prince's account that many
Fell to the ground, unconscious.
They crowded around him, kissed
And embraced him, sick with grief.
The pain could not have been worse
Had he fallen, bleeding, in battle.
He tried to lift their spirits:
"My friends, why such tears?
I haven't been wounded, I'm not
A prisoner. This weeping won't help.
I'm going, yes, but with God's
Blessing I'm bound to return.
I commend you all to Him
And ask that you let me leave:
You're keeping me here too long,
And seeing you weep like this
Wearies me, heart and soul."
He blessed them once more, and they him,

And he made his painful departure.
So Erec went, he
And his wife, not knowing where,
But seeking adventure. "We'll ride
Quickly," he told her. "Be careful,
Whatever you see, not
To say a word. Speak
To me only if
And when I speak to you.
Ride in front, as fast
As you can, and as if you owned
The road." "Good luck, my lord!"
She replied, and led the way,
And was still; neither spoke
A word, but Enide sorrowed
As she went, speaking softly
To herself, so he couldn't hear:
"Wretch!" she murmured. "God,
Who raised you to the height of happiness,
Now drops you, like that! to the dust!
And Fortune, having held out
Her hand, has pulled it back.
Miserable as I am, would it matter
If I dared to speak to my lord?
But what wounds me worst of all
Is how my lord hates me.
And he does, oh, I see it!
Or why refuse to speak?
I'm too afraid to turn
And look in his direction."
As she sighed and suffered,
A knight who lived by robbing

Others rode from the wood,
Together with two companions,
All of them armed. And he liked
The look of the horse she was riding.
"Gentlemen," he said to his friends,
"Just look what's coming our way.
If we can't make the most
Of this, we're three unlucky
Thieves, and shrinking cowards.
Here's this gorgeous lady—
And yet, she may be a girl.
But look at the clothes she's wearing!
What a horse! And that saddle!
I'd guess the harness leather
Alone is worth a fortune.
But what I want is the horse:
You're welcome to all the rest
As long as I get the horse.
Lord! Her knight's already
Lost those treasures; they're mine.
Let me tell you, my friends:
I'll handle him so roughly
He'll hurt all over. Stay here:
I claim the right to tackle
This fellow all by myself."
The others agreed, and he dug in
His spurs, covered himself
With his shield, and left them behind.
It was not the custom, then,
For more than one man at a time
To attack a single knight,
And the world would have branded as traitors

ay who broke that rule.
Seeing the thieves, Enide
Was seized with terrible fear:
"My God!" she thought. "Should I speak?
They'll kill or capture my lord,
They being three and he
Alone. It isn't fair
For a single knight to fight three
At once. And that one's attacking,
Although my lord can't see him.
Lord! Can I sit and say nothing?
Am I such an utter coward?
No, I can't do it,
I have to warn him, that can't
Be wrong." And turning quickly
Toward him, she said, "My lord!
Watch out! Three knights are charging
At you, armed to the teeth.
Be careful! This fills me with fear."
"What?" said Erec. "What?
Do you think so little of me?
How bold you've become, breaking
My prohibition, defying
The command I solemnly gave you.
Well, I'll pardon you once—
But let it happen again
And there'll be no pardon, I warn you."
Then he swung his shield and his spear
Around, and attacked the knight,
Who, seeing him ready, shouted
A challenge, which Erec answered
In kind. Both of them spurred

Their horses, lances ready.
The robber knight struck
At nothing, but Erec's aim
Was perfect, his stroke tremendous:
The robber's shield was split
From top to bottom, nor
Did his mail shirt serve him better,
For Erec smashed it across
His chest, then drove his spear
A foot and a half deep.
When he pulled it out, pivoting
Around, his enemy fell
And was dead, his heart's blood
On the spear. A second knight
Came charging right at Erec,
Riding up from the rear.
Setting his shield in front of him,
Erec attacked at once.
Both shields held high, they drove
Together, shield on shield.
But his enemy's lance broke
In two, while Erec's ran
A quarter of its length through the other's
Body, and he was done with fighting;
Erec tossed him to the ground,
Then turned at an angle and attacked
His friend. And seeing him come,
The third thief broke and ran:
He was too afraid to wait,
Seeking to save himself
In the forest. It did him no good.
Erec came racing after:

"Stop, thief! Stop!
Stand and fight or I'll kill you
Even as you run! You won't
Escape me, now." But the frightened
Man just kept on running,
Fleeing as fast as his horse
Would take him. But Erec caught up
And struck his painted shield
So hard he toppled backward.
These were three thieves who wouldn't
Worry him: one dead, one wounded,
And one left only his legs
To carry him, dropped to the ground.
Erec had all their horses,
Tied together by the reins:
Three very different animals,
One as white as milk,
The second black (but not
Too black), the third dappled.
He led them back to the road,
Where Enide was waiting. He ordered
Her to herd the horses,
Keeping them safely in front of her,
And warned her, fiercely, not
To disobey him, but hold
Her tongue, speaking no word
Whatever without his permission.
"Not one word, my lord,"
She answered, "until you wish it."
On they went, and she held
Her tongue.
They'd gone just half

A mile when they saw, in a valley
Ahead, five knights riding
Toward them, lances at the ready,
Shields held high, gleaming
Helmets laced and tied:
They intended to rob and steal.
They saw the lady, leading
Three horses, coming toward them,
Erec riding behind.
A few quick words, murmured
Among them, were enough to share out
Horses, harnesses, and all,
As if they already owned them.
Greed is evil, vile—
But they fancied nothing stood
In their way, they would have what they wanted.
Yet doing and thinking are different;
Expecting to win isn't winning.
Their plan of attack was like this:
One said he'd take the lady
Or die trying; another
Said he'd take the dappled
Horse, for that would pay him
Well enough for his labor;
The third wanted the black
Horse. Said the fourth, "I'll take
The white!" The fifth wasn't shy,
Declaring he'd settle for Erec's
Arms and armor, and his horse.
Indeed, he'd win them man
For man, and all alone,
If his comrades agreed. Which they cheerfully

Did. So he rode on ahead
—And he rode a first-rate, dashing
Horse. Erec saw him
Yet acted as if he hadn't.
But the moment she saw them coming
Enide's blood went racing;
She was overcome with fear:
"Misery! What can I do?
What can I say? My lord
Has warned me not to make him
Angry by speaking a single
Word, no matter what.
And yet, if they kill my lord
There'll be no one and nothing to help me,
I'll be as good as dead.
Oh God! My lord sees nothing.
Why are you waiting, idiot?
Why worry about that promise?
It's been so long since I said
A thing! And surely these men
Mean to do him harm.
Lord, how can I tell him?
He'll kill me. Then let him kill me!
How can I keep from telling him?"
So she said, softly, "My lord!"
"What? What do you want?"
"Have mercy, my lord! It's just
That five bold men have ridden
Out of the forest, and they frighten me.
I've watched them coming and I'm sure
They propose to pick a fight
With you. Four have hung back,

And the fifth one's coming toward you
As fast as his horse can carry him.
He'll be here any minute.
And those four who stayed behind
Are still so very close;
They could all help if they had to."
He answered, "You've done wrong,
Breaking once again
The silence I laid upon you.
I've always known you thought me
Worth remarkably little.
You'll win no thanks from me,
Giving such warnings. Listen,
And understand: I hate you.
I've told you before, and I tell you
Once more. I'll pardon you
Again, but next time watch out.
Stop looking at me: it makes you
Act like a fool, because
I loathe the words you speak."
Then he turned to the knight who was riding
Directly at him, and attacked.
They fought fiercely. Erec
Struck him so hard that he smashed
The shield hung around
His neck, and cracked his collarbone.
His stirrups broke, and he fell,
Nor was Erec worried he might rise
Once more, with such serious wounds.
Then one of his friends attacked,
And again they fought fiercely.
Erec struck with such force

That his sharp and well-forged weapon
Went under the chin and into
The throat, cutting bones
And muscles, emerging from the back
Of his neck. Hot red blood
Ran both where it entered
And left. His soul fled,
His heart stopped. The next one
Attacked across a ford.
He'd gotten halfway across
When Erec, spurring his horse,
Met him as he reached the bank
And hit him so hard that he fell
Flat, with his horse on top of him.
The animal's weight kept him
From rising, and of course he drowned,
Though the horse struggled so hard
That it finally got to its feet.
So Erec had conquered three of them.
The other two decided
Discretion was better than valor,
And they at least wouldn't fight.
They galloped down the river.
But Erec came chasing after,
Striking from the rear so hard
That the man bent down toward his saddle.
Erec had swung so strongly
That his lance shattered, as his enemy
Collapsed forward on his face.
Erec made him dearly
Regret that spear, broken
On his back. He drew his sword;

The man sat up, which was folly;
For Erec struck him three
Such blows that the sword drank blood,
Slicing away a shoulder,
And the man tumbled to the ground.
Then he swung his sword at the last one,
Who was fleeing as fast as he could,
Awaiting no escort or safe
Conduct, afraid to delay
But unable to escape. Trusting
His horse no longer, he gave
It up, threw away
Sword and lance, and dropped
To the ground. Erec refused
To fight a man with his face
In the dirt. But he bent and collected
The discarded spear, to replace
The one he had broken. Carrying
The lance, he turned back, not
Forgetting the horses: he took
All five and led them to where
His wife was waiting. Herding
These five, and the other three,
Would be serious work. He told her
To hurry and, still, to hold
Her tongue or live to regret it.
She made no reply, remaining
Silent. So on they went,
And all the horses with them.
    They rode until it grew dark,
Seeing no house, no village.
At dusk, he allowed them to shelter

Beneath a tree in a wood.
Erec instructed the lady
To sleep, if she liked, but she said
She wouldn't, it wasn't right,
And she didn't want to; he ought
To sleep, for he was truly
Tired. Erec agreed,
And was pleased. He put his sword
Under his head; she took
Her cloak and covered him well.
He slept, and she watched, not closing
Her eyes the whole night long.
Till morning came, she held
The reins of all eight horses.
And how she criticized
Herself for the words she'd spoken!
She'd been too afraid and excited:
"I haven't suffered even
Half I ought to. Oh miserable
Wretch! See what evil
Your pride and arrogance bring you!
Surely I should have known
There exists no better knight
Than my lord, or indeed his equal.
I knew it—and now I know it
Still better, for I've seen it myself:
He wasn't afraid of three
Or of five! My ungrateful tongue
Should suffer for speaking such swollen
Pride, which shames my heart."
And so she lamented, all
Night long, till dawn arrived,

And Erec awoke, and rose,
And set them along the road,
She in front, he
To the rear. Toward noon they saw
A squire riding out
Of a valley, together with a pair
Of servants carrying biscuits
And wine and five rich cheeses
For those who were cutting hay
In Count Galoain's fields.
The squire was a clever sort:
He saw Erec and the lady
Coming out of the woods,
And knew they had spent the night
Under the trees, and couldn't
Have eaten or drunk, since a day's
Journey in any direction
Would turn up no castle, town,
Or tower, no house or abbey,
No inn or resting place.
He conceived a generous plan,
And changing his path gave them
A courteous greeting, saying,
"My lord, it seems to me
You've spent an unpleasant night,
And surely you can't have slept
Long or well in the forest.
Allow me to offer this white
Biscuit, if you'd care to eat.
I want nothing in return
And ask nothing. These biscuits
Are made from very good wheat,

And I've excellent wine and rich
Cheese, a white tablecloth,
And handsome goblets; if you wish
To breakfast, go no farther.
Here in this shade, under
These elms, lay down your arms
And rest yourself a bit.
Dismount, I beg you, and dine."
Erec dismounted, saying,
"My very good friend, yes,
I will eat, and thanks to you:
I wish to go no farther."
He served them quickly, and well:
First helping the lady down
And having his men see
To the horses, he led them both
To the shade, and seated them there,
Then helped Erec out
Of his helmet, unlacing the heavy
Visor covering his face.
Then he spread the tablecloth
In front of them, on the thick grass,
Brought them biscuits and wine,
And cut and trimmed the cheese.
They were hungry indeed, and ate,
And gladly drank the wine.
The squire attended them well,
Nor were his efforts wasted.
Erec ate and drank,
Then said, polite and generous,
"My friend, allow me, please,
To offer you one of my horses:

Take whichever suits you.
And let me ask, if you care to,
That you ride back into town
And find me some worthy lodging."
The squire replied that he'd gladly
Do whatever Erec
Wanted. Then he walked to the horses,
Untied them and, thanking Erec,
Made the black one his choice.
He mounted, using the left
Stirrup, and rode rapidly
Off into town, where he quickly
Arranged a fine and suitable
Lodging, and as quickly returned.
"Mount, my lord," he said,
"Your lodging awaits you." Erec
Mounted first, and then
His lady. The town was not
Distant; they were soon there.
And their host was delighted to have them,
Giving his guests a hearty
Welcome, offering with open
Hands whatever they needed.
And the squire, having done them
All the honor he could,
Remounted his new horse
And rode to the stable; his path
Took him under the castle
Windows, where the count and three
Of his knights were looking out.
Seeing one of his squires
On such a horse, the lord

Of the castle asked who owned it,
And the squire said it was his.
The count was truly astonished:
"Yours? Where did you get it?"
"A wonderfully noble knight,
My lord, gave me this gift.
I brought him to town; he's taken
Lodgings with a merchant. He's truly
A knight of infinite courtesy:
I've never seen a more handsome
Man—so striking, indeed,
I couldn't come close to telling
Just how he looks and what
He is." Said the count, "Surely
He's no more handsome than I am."
"My lord, truly you're
A handsome, noble man.
This land has never seen
Or given birth to a man
Better looking. And yet,
I have to say that even
Weary from a tight-laced mail shirt
And bruised by blows from combat
With eight strong knights, all
Alone in the forest, knights
He defeated, whose steeds he captured
And led away, he's handsomer
Still. His lady is with him,
And she, my lord, is so lovely
That no woman alive has half
Her beauty." Hearing this news,
The count was anxious to see

For himself how true it might be:
"I know nothing of your knight.
Take me to his lodging and show me
Whether you're dreaming or telling
The truth." Said the squire, "Gladly,
My lord. It's not very far;
Please follow, I'll lead the way."
"By God, I'm dying to see him,"
Said the count, and came down to the courtyard.
The squire dismounted and helped
His master onto his horse,
Then ran in front, to announce
To Erec that the count was making
A call. As usual, Erec's
Lodgings were lavishly furnished:
Candles flared in every
Corner, and a host of lamps
Were burning. The count had carefully
Kept his escort to a mere
Three. Erec rose
To greet him, like a well-bred man,
Saying, "Welcome, my lord!"
And the count returned his greeting.
Seating themselves on soft
White cushions, they began to converse.
The count offered, and begged
Erec to accept, repayment
For the cost of his lodgings, but Erec,
Courteous yet firm, assured him
He had more than enough and thus
Needed to trouble no one.
They spoke of this and that,

But as they talked, the count
Kept glancing off to the side,
For he'd seen Erec's wife
And been so struck by her beauty
That, truly, he thought of nothing
Else. His eyes kept wandering
Toward her, more and more
Attracted, until he was burning
With love. He concealed that longing,
And asked Erec for leave
To address her: "A permission depending
From first to last on your pleasure,
My lord. It would please me to sit
Beside her and make her welcome.
I come in friendship, as you see,
So I trust you'll not be offended:
I wish no more than to pledge
My service, as she may desire."
Erec, as far from jealous
As from home, suspected nothing:
"My lord, that's quite all right.
Talk and laugh as you like.
I see no harm: I grant you
Cheerful permission to greet her."
The lady was seated as far
Away as the length of two lances;
The count went and sat
Close by, on a wooden stool.
Polite and pleasant and sensible,
The lady turned in his
Direction. "Oh," he said,
"It pains me, seeing you live

In such squalor! It hurts me deeply.
Believe me, you could win fame
And honor and wealth, if you liked.
Beauty like yours deserves
Enormous honor, immense
Respect. I'd make you my love,
If you pleased, if that made you happy;
You'd be my lady love
And queen of all I own.
Since I've been good enough
To ask for your love, you can't
Refuse me. It's perfectly clear
Your lord has no use for you,
And no love. You'd have a good
Husband, if you came to me."
"Don't trouble yourself, my lord,"
Said Enide. "It's out of the question.
Ah! I'd rather remain
Unborn, or be burned in flaming
Briars and my ashes thrown
To the wind, than betray my lord
In any way, or even
Dream of treachery and treason!
You've done me a grave injustice,
Demanding such a terrible thing:
I'd never, never do it."
The count's anger flared:
"You can't stoop to my love,
Woman? You're far too proud!
I ask, I even beg you,
And you won't do what I want?
Women are known to be prideful;

The more they're asked, the more
They deny, but those who treat them
Badly are much better served.
Yet let me tell you, here
And now: you'll do as I want
Or a sword-blade will settle the affair.
One way or another, right
Or wrong, your husband will die
In battle, in front of your eyes."
"My lord," said Enide, "you neglect
A better and easier path.
How terribly wicked it would be,
How vile and treacherous, to kill him
Like that. But calm yourself,
Dear sir: I'll do as you wish.
You can have me; I'll
Be yours, and gladly. It wasn't
Pride that made me speak
As I did, but my need to know
If you truly spoke from the heart
And meant what you said. But I couldn't
For all the world let you
Do such a traitorous thing.
My lord has no suspicions
Of you: to kill him would be
A vile and miserable deed,
And the guilt would fall on me
As well. Every mouth
Would say I had you do it.
Wait till tomorrow morning,
When my lord is ready to rise
And then confront him as you please

And incur no guilt. That's better."
The mouth's words are never
The heart's thoughts. "My lord,"
She said, "believe me, be patient.
Tomorrow, send your knights
And your soldiers to take me by force.
My lord, who's brave and strong,
Will try to protect me. Then kill him
However you choose—in combat,
If you like, or stab him, or cut off
His head. I'm sick and tired
Of living like this, and to tell you
The truth, I'm sick of him
And weary of having him with me.
Oh, I already feel you
Naked in my bed, breast
To breast. And when it comes
To that, you'll know how I love you."
The count replied, "Till then,
Lady! You were born lucky.
How well you'll be treated here!"
"My lord," she said, "I believe it.
But all the same, I want you
To swear you'll always love me,
Or else I can never trust you."
The count replied, bursting
With joy, "Lady, you have
My word, as a true and faithful
Count. You'll always be treated
Well. Don't worry yourself:
You'll always have what you want."
And so she had his promise,

But she knew how much it was worth,
Except for saving her lord.
She knew just how to intoxicate
Fools with a word, when she had to:
And how much better to lie
Than see her lord cut
To pieces? The count left her,
Commending her to God
A hundred times, but she knew
How little his words were worth.
Erec had no suspicion
Anyone was plotting his death,
But God above could save him—
And it seems to me He will.
All the same, his peril
Was great and real, yet he knew
Nothing. The count, meanwhile,
Played his evil part,
Intending to murder the husband
And steal the wife, but saying
"I commend you to God" as he left.
"And I you," said Erec.
And thus they said their farewells.
  It was already late at night.
Beds for husband and wife
Had been made in a side room.
Erec lay in one,
And Enide, deeply troubled,
Lay in the other, tossing
And turning all night long,
Kept awake with worry
For her lord, well aware

That the count was capable of any
And every sort of evil.
And she knew that once he had
Erec in his power, her husband
Was almost as good as dead.
What could she find to comfort her?
So she lay in the dark, waiting
For dawn, hoping that before
It was light, if her husband believed her,
They'd have taken their leave, and the count
Would have plotted for nothing, and neither
She nor her husband would be
In his power. Erec slept
Long, suspecting nothing,
And with daylight almost upon them
She knew it was dangerous to wait.
Her heart was neither deceitful
Nor false: as a loyal lady,
And true, her feelings for her lord
Were tender. So she rose, and dressed,
And went to her lord, and woke him:
"For pity's sake, my lord!
Let's leave this place, and quickly,
For you've been completely betrayed,
And for no reason, no cause.
The count has proven himself
A traitor: if he finds you here
You'll never leave alive;
He'll tear you to pieces. He hates you
On my account; he wants me.
May God in His infinite goodness
Keep you from being captured

Or killed! He meant to kill you
Last night. But I made him believe
I'd come to him and love him.
He'll be here soon, you'll see;
He means to take me, and keep me,
And kill you, here, if he can."
Then Erec truly saw
How loyally loving his wife was.
"Lady," he said, "order
Our horses saddled at once,
And wake up our host, and tell him
To come to me here. Treachery
Leaves us no time to lose!"
Then the horses were quickly saddled,
And the lady summoned their host.
Erec put on his armor.
The host appeared, saying,
"Why are you hurrying, my lord,
Rising at such an hour,
Even before it's dawn?"
Erec answered he had far
To go that day, a long
And difficult journey, so he wanted
To be ready; it weighed on his mind.
And he added, "Sir, you haven't
Drawn up my bill. You've treated
Me well, and done me honor,
And deserve to be well paid.
Shall we call it quits in return
For the seven horses I have
In your stables? It's more then enough,
And they're yours. Right now, I'm afraid,

I couldn't give you another
Bit." This gift delighted
The merchant, who threw himself
At Erec's feet and thanked him.
Then Erec mounted, said
Farewell, and left—but not
Before he warned Enide
That whatever she saw on the way
She should not dream of addressing
A single word to him.
And then a hundred knights
In armor entered the house,
All deeply disappointed,
Not finding Erec at home.
The count understood at once
That the lady had tricked him. Seeing
The horses' hoofprints, he ordered
His men to give chase and, crying
Threats against Erec, declared,
If only he could catch him,
Nothing could stop him, now,
From cutting off his head.
"Curses on any man
Who refuses to spur his horse!
Whoever brings me his head,
This knight I loathe and detest,
Will have served me well and be well
Rewarded." They galloped off,
Wild with rage at those
They'd never seen and who'd never
Said or done a thing
To them. They rode so hard

That just at the edge of a forest
They saw Erec before
The trees hid him. Hungry
For a quarrel, none of them stopped.
Hearing the sound of horses
And weapons, Enide looked
And saw the valley teeming
With riders. And seeing them come
She couldn't keep from speaking:
"My lord, my lord!" she cried.
"This count doesn't just chase you,
He sets an army on your trail!
Ride faster, my lord, ride faster!
We're right at the edge of this forest.
We can still escape them: they're far
Behind, there's still enough time.
But jogging along as we are
We'll never get away,
And they're so many, and you're
Just one." "You don't think much
Of me," he said, "always
Defying my orders. What
Can I say to make you behave?
Ah me, if God is merciful
And I leave this combat alive,
You'll pay for these errors, and dearly,
Unless I'm moved to forgive you."
And then he swung around
And saw the count's steward
Leading the attack, on a strong,
Swift horse, making an open
Challenge from four bowshots

Distant. His armor and weapons
Were good, and nothing was mortgaged.
Counting up his enemies,
Erec saw a hundred
Or more. He thought he'd begin
By stopping the one in front.
They clashed, razor-sharp spear points
Beating on shields, and Erec
Drove the gleaming steel
Of his lance deep in the steward's
Body. Neither his shield
Nor his mail shirt worked any better
Than a bolt of blue silk. The count
Was next. The story assures us
He was truly a powerful fighter,
But wielding only a spear
And a shield, so sure of himself
He refused anything more.
And his courage was clear, for he galloped
At Erec hundreds of yards
In front of his men. And seeing
The count thus open and exposed,
Erec attacked. Not a bit
Afraid, the count charged on
And quickly struck the first blow,
Hitting Erec so hard
On the chest that his stirrups would
Have snapped, had they not been well tied.
The shield-wood cracked, and the spear point
Passed straight through, but Erec's
Mail shirt, so beautifully worked,
Saved him from certain death:

Not a single link gave way.
The count was strong, and his spear
Shattered. Then Erec struck him
So fiercely on his yellow shield
That the lance pierced his stomach
A yard or more deep, and the count
Fell from his horse like a stone.
Erec rode back as fast
As he'd come, wasting no time,
Heading straight for the forest,
Making his horse gallop.
So there was Erec, safe
In the woods, and the others stopped
In the middle of the field where the bodies
Were lying. They shouted and swore,
Declaring they'd keep up the chase
For a day or two or three,
Until they caught and killed him.
The count, his belly bleeding
Freely, heard what they said.
He pulled himself up, barely
Opening his eyes: he realized,
Now, what an evil thing
He'd been doing. He called to his knights,
Commanding them to stop:
"Gentlemen," he said, "among
The lot of you there isn't
One, no matter how noble,
Strong or brave, who's good
Enough to catch him. Go back
At once! I'm guilty of evil
Deeds, and they weigh on my heart.

The lady who tricked me is wise
And courteous, bold and brave.
Her beauty set me to burning,
And because I wanted her
So badly I tried to kill
Her husband and carry her off
By force. I deserve to suffer,
And suffering has come to me, for I
Was a traitor, disloyal, false,
Crazed by my wild treason.
No man born of woman
Is a better knight than this one:
I'll try never to raise
My hand against him. And again:
I command you to return, one
And all." Their hearts sad,
They obeyed. They bore the steward's
Body; they carried the count
On his shield—and in spite of his serious
Wounds, he lived a long life.
Which was how Erec was saved.
  His wife riding in front of him,
They galloped along a road
With hedges and trees on either
Side, leading to a small
Meadow, cleared and open.
And where the fenced-in wood
Ended, they found a great
Deep moat, and then a bridge,
And a tall tower surrounded
All around with a wall.
They rattled over the bridge,

But before they'd even crossed it
They were seen, from high above,
By the lord of the tower. This lord,
Let me tell you, was wonderfully
Small of body, a dwarf,
But large of heart, and brave.
As Erec rode across,
He came down from his tower and ordered
A saddle embossed with golden
Lions to be put on a huge
Chestnut horse. He ordered
His shield, and his stiff, straight spear,
His honed and polished sword,
His brightly gleaming helmet,
His triple-mailed armor and mail shirt,
So that having seen a knight
Cross his battle lines
He could test his strength, and his skill,
Until the one or the other
Had won or given up.
His every command was obeyed
And as soon as the horse was saddled
And ready, a squire led it
To their waiting master, and others
Brought him his weapons and armor.
The tiny knight rode out
The gate, as fast as he could,
And all alone. Erec
Was riding up a slope.
The tiny knight came dashing
Down it; he'd started at the top,
His proud, excited horse

Raising a fearful racket
As its iron hooves struck
Against the rocks, mashing them
Finer than a mill grinds wheat;
It ran as if candles
Flared in its every nerve,
And each of its four feet
Had been set on fire and was burning.
Enide was terrified,
Almost falling off
Her horse, fainting, unconscious;
Every single vein
In her body was pulsing, throbbing:
The skin of a cold corpse
Would have gleamed as pale and white.
She trembled in misery and despair—
For how could she disobey
Again, how could she dare,
When silence was so strongly commanded?
Her mind wavered back
And forth, she could not choose
The proper path: to speak,
To warn her lord, or be silent?
She tried to think, to decide,
Sometimes her lips parting,
Her tongue beginning to move,
But her voice unable to speak,
Fear snapping her teeth
Together, locking the words
In her mouth, only able
To control herself by shutting
The gates of speech. She fought

With herself, she struggled, thinking:
"Losing my lord would be terrible,
Painful: that's for sure.
A horrible loss. So:
Can I simply speak as I will?
Impossible. Why? I don't dare,
I'd make him terribly angry,
And if I make him angry
My lord's likely to leave me
All alone in this wood,
Worse off than ever. Worse off?
Why should it make any difference?
I'll never need to hunt
For trouble, as long as I live,
If my lord's able to escape,
Now, without receiving
Some mortal wound. But still,
If I never warn my lord
About this knight, dashing
Down the hill, desperate
To kill him, then he'll be dead
Before he notices. I've already
Waited too long! I'm forbidden
To speak—but why should that stop me?
Clearly, my lord's so lost
In thought, he's even forgotten
Himself! I've got to warn him."
She spoke. And though he poured out
Threats, he hadn't the heart
To hurt her, seeing as clearly
As he did how deeply she loved him
And he, in turn, loved her.

So he spurred his horse and attacked
The knight who'd attacked him first.
They met at the end of the bridge,
Each wielding his lance
Against the other, striking
With every bit of his strength.
The shields hung from their necks
Helped them as much as two bits
Of bark: leather and wood
Split, chain mail broke,
As each jabbed his spear point
Into his enemy's belly
And both horses fell
To the ground. Both of the men
Were strong; neither was mortally
Wounded. Tossing their spears
Aside, they drew out swords
And clashed angrily. They hacked
And slashed, neither holding
Back or sparing the other,
Raining so many massive
Strokes that helmets sparked
And swords recoiled, shields
Were sliced to shreds, mail shirts
Battered, split, cracked,
So that many blows reached
Bare flesh, and slowly their strength
Faded, their arms grew weak.
Indeed, had both swords
Remained intact, neither
Man could have asked for a breather,
Nor could the combat have ended

Except with one of them dead.
Enide had been watching the battle,
Almost insane with misery.
Anyone seeing her suffer,
Twisting her hands, tearing
Her hair, weeping bitterly,
Would know how loyal a lady
She was, and only the hardest
Heart could fail to feel pity.
They struck each other immense
Blows: from nine in the morning
Till three they fought fiercely,
And no one watching could ever
Have seen that either was a better
Knight in any way.
Erec summoned strength
And courage, swinging his sword
Through his enemy's helmet
To the metal hood beneath;
It broke, but the man stood firm
And fought on, his sword striking
Erec's shield so fiercely
That the metal-plaited wood
Cracked his sword, so costly
And fine. He was wild with fury,
Seeing it broken, and threw
Away the fragment still
In his hand, threw it as far
As he could. And then he was frightened,
Needing to retreat, for a knight
Without a weapon can't fight
A battle or sustain an assault.

And when Erec pursued him, the knight
Begged in God's great name
Not to be slaughtered: "Have mercy,
Noble knight! Don't treat me
Cruelly: now that my sword
Has failed me, you have the power
And the means to kill me, and I
Have no way to defend myself."
Erec replied, "Admit,
Then, in unmistakable
Terms, that you're beaten and conquered.
That's all I ask. Surrender
Yourself, and you're safe from attack."
The knight was silent. Seeing
How he delayed, and wanting
To frighten him into surrender,
Erec raised his sword
And ran right at him. The knight
Was terror-stricken, crying,
"Mercy, my lord! You've won,
I'm helpless, I have no choice."
"That's not enough," said Erec.
"You can't get off so easily.
Tell me who and what
You are, and then I'll tell you."
"You're right, my lord," he said.
"I am the king of this land,
And the men who owe me tribute
And loyalty are Irish.
My name is Guivret the Dwarf;
I've power and wealth in abundance.
Wherever you look, in every

Direction, barons with lands
Near mine obey my rule
And do as I wish. All
My neighbors fear me, no matter
How proud they are or how brave.
And I long to be your comrade
And friend forever." Erec
Replied, "I too can boast
Of my ancient, noble family:
I'm Erec, son of King Lac.
My father rules in Outer
Wales, and owns rich cities,
Fine homes, and many powerful
Castles. No king or emperor
Owns more, except King Arthur,
To whom no living man
Can ever hope to compare."
Hearing this, Guivret
Was astonished: "My lord, I'm amazed!
No joy I've ever known
Has delighted me more than meeting
You. Please: treat
My land and goods as your own.
You'll honor me in accepting.
And as long as you wish to remain
You'll be my lord and my king.
But both of us need a physician
First, and one of my homes
Is a very few miles away.
Allow me to lead you there
And have our wounds attended
To." "Thank you for those gracious

Words," said Erec. "I'm grateful.
But I can't go. All
I ask of you is this:
If ever I find myself
In trouble, and you hear of my
Distress, don't forget me
But come to my aid." "My lord,
You have my pledge and my promise
That as long as I live you'll have
All the help I can offer
If ever you need it." "There's nothing
Else I want from you,"
Said Erec. "You've promised everything.
If your actions match your words
You'll be my friend and my comrade."
And they kissed each other as friends.
No battle brutally hard
Was ever broken off
So sweetly, in mutual grace
And affection, each of them tearing
Broad bandages from their shirts
And binding the other's wounds.
And when each had taken care
Of the other, they commended themselves
To God, and parted, as follows:
 Guivret stayed where he was,
And Erec went on his way,
In sore need of ointments
To put on his wounds. They rode
Hard, he and his wife,
And, coming to open country,
Saw a great forest

Full of leaping stags
And bucks, and savage beasts,
And every animal alive.
Here, King Arthur and his queen,
And the best of his barons, had come
Hunting, intending, for their pleasure
And sport, to linger three
Or four days; the king had ordered
Pavilions brought, and tents,
And awnings against the sun,
And his servants had set them out.
Sir Gawain, who'd had enough
Of riding and wanted only
Rest, was sleeping in the king's
Tent; on an elm in front of it
Hung a shield bearing
His coat of arms and his ash-wood
Lance; and from a branch,
Employing famous Gringolet's
Reins, he let saddle and bridle
Hang. The horse was grazing
Quietly when Kay, the king's
Steward, came hurrying up
And, making merry at Gawain's
Expense, mounted (for no one
Was there to stop him). Having
The horse, he also took
The lance and shield hanging
Nearby. And then he galloped
Gringolet along a valley,
Where as it happened he met
Erec. Now Erec knew

Sir Kay, as he also knew
Both the horse and the weapons,
But Kay didn't know
Erec, for the battle markings
Were gone, and the painted shield
Had suffered so many blows
From sword and spear that the coat
Of arms had disappeared.
Erec's lady, unwilling
To be seen, quickly draped
Her veil across her face,
As if against the dust
Or heat. Kay came pressing
Forward, cutting off Erec's
Path, silently seizing
His reins. And holding the horse
In place, he asked, arrogantly,
"Knight, I want you to tell me
Who you are and where
You're from." "You must be a fool,"
Said Erec. "I'll tell you nothing."
"Don't be angry," Kay said.
"I ask with your interests at heart.
It isn't hard to see
You're badly wounded. So stay
With me tonight. Come,
I'll treat you well, I offer you
Honor and comfort. Rest
Is clearly just what you need.
King Arthur and his queen are here
Close by, in a wood, lodged
In tents and pavilions. I ask you

In the best of faith to come
With me and visit my king
And his queen: they'll entertain you
Royally and show you honor."
"How well you talk," said Erec,
"But nothing could make me join you.
You know nothing of my needs;
I've many more miles to go.
Let go; I've lingered too long,
There's plenty of daylight left."
Said Kay, "You're talking nonsense.
Why this silly refusal?
I expect you'll change your mind—
You and your lady, you'll come,
All right, willy-nilly,
Like it or not, like a priest
Summoned by bishops. You're bound
To endure a nasty night,
Let me tell you, unless
You take my advice. And you can't
Refuse, I've got you in my hand."
Erec answered disdainfully,
"You're crazy, fellow, trying
To force me to follow behind you.
I refuse. You made no challenge;
You had no business seizing
My reins without a challenge
To put me on guard." Then he put
His hand on his sword and said,
"Fellow, let go of those reins!
Leave us! I tell you, you're
A haughty, conceited fool!

I warn you: keep those reins
In your hand, and you'll feel my sword.
Let go!" And Kay released him,
Drew himself off a bit,
Then galloped rapidly back,
Shouting an angry challenge
As the distance narrowed. Far
Too noble to kill a knight
Wearing no armor, Erec
Turned his spear so only
The handle would hit him, but leveled
So hard a blow on the fattest
Part of the shield that it smashed
Against Kay's forehead and pinned
His arms to his chest and stretched him
Full length on the ground. And then
Erec took Gringolet
By the reins and led him to Enide,
Intending to lead him off.
But Kay, a skilled flatterer,
Sought to keep the horse
With the softest words, saying,
"Friend, as God is my witness,
I have no right to that horse:
It belongs to one of the best
And most famous knights in the world,
Gawain the Brave. I ask you
In his name and for his sake
To give me Gringolet back.
Let me serve as your messenger:
So wise and noble a deed
Will do you infinite honor."

"Take the horse," said Erec,
"And bring him back to his owner.
It would be wrong of me
To deprive my lord Gawain."
Kay mounted the horse
And rode to the king's tent,
And told him what had happened.
And Arthur summoned Gawain,
Saying, "My fine nephew,
For the sake of all that's noble
In you, ride right after him,
Ask him gently what
He is, and why he's here,
And if, somehow, you can get him
To think of making a visit,
By all means do so." So Gawain
Mounted Gringolet
And followed by a pair of servants
Soon caught up to Erec,
But did not know who he was.
Each of them gave the other
A careful, courteous greeting.
Then Gawain, clearly a knight
Of enormous breeding, declared,
"My lord, King Arthur sent me
After you, down this road.
The king and queen send
You greetings, and ask most kindly
That you come and enjoy their company:
They'd like to help you, they mean you
No harm, and they're very close by."
Erec replied, "My deepest

Thanks to the king and the queen,
And to you; you're plainly a wellborn,
Well-bred man. Right now
I'm not in the best of health,
I've been badly wounded all over
My body and can't afford
To go out of my way for lodging.
Please don't trouble yourself;
I thank you; please go back."
  Gawain was nobody's fool.
Drawing aside, he bent
To a servant's ear and, whispering,
Told him to ride directly
To the king, advising Arthur
To take down his tents and pavilions
And carry them two or three miles
Away, then set them up
Again, right in the middle
Of the road. "And there is where
The king must sleep, if he wants
To meet and entertain
The very best knight, to my mind,
Anyone's ever seen,
For nothing could make this knight
Leave the road and take shelter."
The servant left, and delivered
His message. The king struck
His tents at once, and had
Packhorses carry them off.
Then he mounted Aubagu,
And the queen, too, prepared
To ride on her white horse.

And all this time, Gawain
Worked at delaying Erec,
Who finally said, "Sir:
Yesterday I traveled
Farther than today. You're bothering
Me: please leave. You've made me
Lose the better part
Of this day." And Gawain answered,
"Ah, let me stay a while
Longer, and ride at your side.
There's plenty of daylight left."
And they talked so much that Arthur's
Servants were able to set up
The tents in front of them, and Erec
Saw them. And now he knew
He was obliged to accept this lodging.
"Ah, ah! Gawain," he said,
"You're far too clever for me:
You've tricked me into staying.
And now, because you've made
This happen, I'll tell you my name:
I've nothing to gain by concealment.
I am Erec, your old
Friend and companion." Hearing
His name, Gawain hugged him,
Then lifted off his helmet
And untied the brace at his neck,
And Erec did the same for him.
Then Gawain left him, saying,
"My friend, this will be welcome
News to my lord and his queen.
Let me go and make them

Both exceedingly happy.
But first, allow me to greet
And embrace and comfort my lady
Enide, your wife. The queen
Will surely want to see her
At once. Just yesterday
I heard her speaking your lady's
Name." Approaching Enide,
He asked her how the journey
Had gone and how she was.
She answered like a well-bred woman:
"My lord, all is well.
My only concern is for
My husband: it worries me,
Seeing him wounded all over."
Gawain replied, "And it worries
Me. I saw at once
That his face was pale and colorless.
It would have made me weep,
Seeing such pain and pallor,
But joy extinguishes sorrow.
Having him back brought me
Such pleasure that pain was forgotten.
If you please, continue exactly
As before; I'll ride like the wind
And inform the king and queen
You're close behind me." They parted;
He came to the king's tent:
"My lord," he said, "You'll both
Be delighted, you and my lady:
Erec and his wife are coming."
Delighted indeed, the king

Jumped up: "By God, but I'm happy!
You couldn't have brought me news
I was gladder to hear." And then
The king and queen left
Their tent, and at once saw Erec
Approaching. Seeing the king,
Erec quickly dismounted
And Enide came down from her horse.
They were greeted by the king, and embraced,
And the queen, too, sweetly
Kissed and hugged them both.
Everyone there was happy.
Right where he stood, servants
Removed Erec's armor,
But seeing his many wounds
Their joy was turned into sorrow.
Arthur sighed profoundly,
Then called for a magic ointment
Prepared by his sister Morgana
For the king's particular use,
A compound so wonderfully mixed
That once spread on a wound—
Muscle or bone, it made
No difference—in just a week
That wound was completely healed,
Provided only the ointment
Was reapplied each day.
This magic ointment was brought
To the king, much to Erec's
Relief. It was rubbed on his wounds,
And his bandages carefully retied.
The king took husband and wife

By the hand and led them inside,
Declaring that solely for love
Of Erec he'd decided to spend
A full two weeks in that forest,
Until all the wounds had been healed.
And Erec thanked the king,
Saying, "My lord, none
Of my wounds pains me so much
That I'm ready to give up my journey.
No one can hold me back.
I wish to leave early
Tomorrow, at the latest, just
As the sun begins to appear."
Shaking his head, the king
Replied, "I deeply regret
This strange unwillingness.
It's perfectly clear you're in pain.
Remaining here is the path
Of wisdom—for what a shame
It would be if you died in this forest.
My good sweet friend, stay
At least until you're well."
"Enough!" said Erec. "I started
This journey and I mean to complete it.
Nothing can keep me here."
Perceiving that not a word
He said could convince the knight,
Arthur gave up the attempt
And ordered tables set out
At once and supper brought.
His servants hurried to obey him.
 It was a Saturday night,

And they dined on fish and fruit,
Perch and pike, salmon
And thick-lipped trout, followed
By pears both fresh and cooked.
As soon as supper was done
Beds were called for, and brought.
The king dearly loved
Erec and gave him a bed
To himself, so no one lying
Too close might touch his wounds.
Erec's lodgings were superb,
That night. And Enide slept
Close by, together with the queen,
Lying under an ermine
Blanket. All were at rest,
Tranquil till morning came.
Erec awoke at dawn,
Rose from his bed, and prepared
To leave, ordering his horse
Saddled and his arms and armor
Brought. He was quickly obeyed.
The king and all his knights
Urged him, once more, to stay,
But their words were a waste of breath:
Nothing could hold him back.
Weeping and wailing began—
Such a wild burst of sorrow
You'd have thought they were watching him die.
He put on his armor; Enide
Stood waiting. They were ready, and everyone
Mourned, sure he would never
Return. Rushing from their tents,

They called for their horses, intending
To ride along as an escort.
But Erec said, "Be calm.
No one needs to come with me.
I thank you all. Go back."
His horse was brought, and he mounted
Quickly, wasting no time;
He took up his shield and his spear.
He commended them all to God,
And they did the same for him.
Enide mounted. And they left.
They rode through the forest, not stopping,
And then, at six o'clock,
As they rode along they heard,
Far off, the voice of a girl
Crying out in distress.
Erec understood that cry:
He knew, the moment it reached
His ears, that the woman was desperate
For help and deeply frightened.
He called to Enide, quickly:
"Lady, there's a girl here
In this wood, crying as she goes.
And it seems to me, hearing
Her voice, she's badly in need
Of help. I'll gallop over
And see what I can do.
Dismount here. I'm off:
Wait for me right where you are."
"Gladly, my lord," she said.
She stayed alone; he went
By himself and quickly found

The girl, running through the woods,
Crying because her beloved
Had been carried off by a pair
Of giants who were handling him savagely.
She was clawing at her hair as she ran,
Ripping her clothes, tearing
The rosy skin of her face.
Astonished at the sight, Erec
Asked her to tell him, please,
Why she wept and lamented.
She sobbed and wept, and told him,
Through her tears: "My lord,
There's nothing strange in my sorrow,
For I'd rather be dead than alive.
My life is worthless, now,
For a pair of cruel, wicked
Giants, my beloved's mortal
Enemies, have taken him prisoner.
Oh Lord! How can a weak
And miserable woman help
The best of all living knights,
The kindest of all, and most noble?
Truly, his life is at stake:
They'll kill him, I know they will,
And he'll die a miserable death.
In the name of God, oh noble
Knight, save my beloved
If you possibly can, save him!
You'll find them pretty quickly,
They haven't gone very far."
"Lady," said Erec, "I'll ride
After them, because you've asked,

And I promise to do whatever
I can: either I'll
Become a prisoner, too,
Or else I'll bring him back.
If only the giants let
Him live until I find them,
I'll set my strength against theirs."
"Oh noble knight," she said,
"I'll be your servant forever,
If you bring me back my love.
May God bless you. Oh hurry,
Hurry, I beg you!" "Tell me
Which way they went." "That way,
My lord. You can see their tracks."
Erec told her to wait
Where she was, and set off at a gallop.
The girl blessed him, in the name
Of the Lord, sweetly praying
To God to give this knight
Strength enough to defeat
Those who were hurting her lover.
   Quickly, Erec tracked them,
Spurring his horse. He rode
Hard and finally spied
The giants up ahead,
About to leave the wood.
With them he saw a naked,
Barefoot knight on a packhorse,
Bound both hands and feet
As if he'd been caught stealing.
And he saw that the giants carried
No lances or shields or swords,

Or any weapons except
Clubs and whips, which they'd used
To beat and lash their prisoner
Until the skin on his back
Was sliced open to the bone.
Blood ran so freely
Along his sides that the packhorse
He rode was bloody all over,
Even down to his belly.
Erec came galloping up,
Alone, shocked and dismayed,
Seeing the captive knight
So savagely treated. He reached them
In a meadow, where one wood ended
And before another began.
"Gentlemen," he said, "for what
Crime are you treating this man
So horribly, leading him like
A thief? This is too much!
You're handling him like a criminal
Caught in the very act.
And to see a knight all naked,
Bound both hand and foot,
And cruelly beaten, is shameful,
A vile and offensive sight.
I ask you, politely, as honest
Men, to hand him over
To me. And I make no threats."
"Hey, is it any business
Of yours? You're crazy, asking
Anything of us! If you think
It's wrong, just try and fix it!"

"It makes me sick to see it,"
Said Erec. "You'll have to fight
To keep him. And since you've said
The decision is mine, and whoever
Wins can have him, step forward!
Before you take him further
You'll have to trade blows with me."
"Fellow," they said, "you're really
Crazy, wanting to fight
With us. Even if there
Were four of you, you'd still
Do as well as a lamb with two wolves."
"Who knows?" Erec replied.
"If the sky falls, and the earth
Cracks, we'll catch a lot
Of skylarks. People who rely
On boasts aren't worth much.
Get ready, I'm coming after you!"
The giants were strong, and savage;
Each of them carried a great square
Club in his closed fist.
Erec charged them, lance
At the ready, not afraid
Of either one, for all
Their arrogant bluster. He struck
The first one right in the eye,
And his spear drove through the skull
So that brains and blood both
Poured out the back. And he fell
Dead, his heart failed.
It troubled the second giant,
Seeing the first one dead,

And well it might. Angry,
And wanting revenge, he charged,
Raising his club with both hands,
Intending to bash in Erec's
Head before he could cover it.
But Erec saw the blow
Coming, and took it on his shield.
But the giant had swung so fiercely
That Erec was stunned, almost
Toppled off his horse
And rolled along the ground.
But he held his shield high;
It rang from the force of the blow.
And the giant raised his club
Again, still aiming for the head,
But Erec's sword was ready
And he swung it so hard that the giant's
Health was hardly improved:
It hit him right in the head
And split him all the way down
To his saddle. His guts spilled out,
His body tumbled to the ground
And lay there, cut in half.
And the captive knight cried
With joy, thanking God
For sending him such a savior.
Erec untied him, helped him
Dress himself, then mounted him
On one of the giants' horses,
Leading the other by its reins.
Then Erec asked him his name,
And the former captive said,

"Good knight, you are now
My lord, my master in everything
By right and reason together,
For my life belongs to you,
Who saved it before they could snatch
The soul right out of my body.
What lucky chance, my sweet
Savior, sent you from God
To save me, pluck me out
Of my enemies' hands, rescue
My body with your bravery? My lord,
Let me do you homage: I wish
To follow you the rest
Of my life, go wherever
You go, and serve you always."
Seeing the passion with which
The former captive wished
To serve him, if he could, Erec
Said, "My friend, I can't
Accept your service, but there's
Something you need to know:
I came to your aid because
Of the prayers, and the tears, of the woman
Who loves you, for I found her weeping
In this wood. She sobbed and cried
For you, and her heart ached.
Let me make her a present:
You. And having brought you
Back, I'll go on my way,
Alone; you can't come with me.
But although I can't accept
Your company, I should like to know

Who you are." "As you please, my lord.
If you wish to know my name
I have no right to withhold it.
Good sir, I'm Cadoc of Cabruel—
And there you have my name.
But now, before you leave me,
I'd like to know, if I may,
Where you come from and who
You are, and where I may hope
To find you again, when you're gone."
"My friend, I shouldn't tell you,"
Said Erec. "Let's say no more!
But if you're searching for something
To bring me honor, go
As quickly as you possibly can
To my lord, King Arthur, who's hard
At work hunting in this forest,
In that direction, only
A couple of miles away.
Go to him now, and say
You were sent to see him by the man
He entertained and was kind to,
There in his tent last night.
Hide nothing from him of the pain
And sorrow you and your lady
And your body might have known.
I'm well-beloved at court,
And if you'll bear me witness
You'll do me an honorable service.
Ask, and they'll tell you who
I am: no one else
Will." "Whatever you order,

My lord," said Cadoc, "I will do.
Don't be afraid I'll fail you.
I'll gladly go to Arthur
And tell the king exactly
How you fought this battle
On my account." And as
They spoke, they rode along
Until they came to where
Erec had left the girl
Waiting. And she was wonderfully
Happy, seeing her lover
Return, as she had not believed
He would. And giving her Cadoc's
Hand, he said, "Be happy,
Lady, not sad, for here
Is your lover, rejoicing." She answered him
Well: "My lord, you've conquered
Us both. Our duty, now,
Can only be to serve
And honor you as best
We can. Yet who could repay
Even a half of what
You've given us?" Erec
Answered, "My sweet friend,
I ask for no reward.
I commend you both to God;
I've lingered longer than I should."
Then he swung his horse around
And rode away as fast
As he could. And Cadoc of Cabruel,
Together with his lady, went
To carry the news to Arthur

And his queen. Erec galloped
Down the road, and at last
Arrived where he'd left his own
Lady, half sick with fear,
Sure that he meant to leave her
All alone in that wood.
And Erec, too, was afraid
That someone might have found her
There, unprotected,
And taken her away,
Which was why he rode hard.
But the day had been so hot,
And his armor had weighed so heavily,
That all his wounds opened,
And his bandages broke, and he bled
Freely, with nothing to hold back
The blood. And then he arrived
Where Enide had been left to wait.
How joyful she was, seeing
Her husband coming! But she could not
See the pain he was suffering,
For his whole body was bathed
In blood, and his heart had almost
Stopped beating. Down a small hill
He rode, then dropped like a falling
Log across his horse's
Neck, and tried to straighten,
But slipped from his saddle, losing
His grip and falling flat
On his face like a corpse. And oh!
Watching him tumble down
Was a terrible sight: she ran

To him, not hiding her sorrow,
Shrieking, wringing her hands,
Ripping away her dress
And baring her breast, tearing
Out her hair, clawing
Bloody lines along
Her tender face. "God!"
She cried, "Oh sweet good Lord!
How can you let me live?
Oh Death, come kill me, I'm yours!"
And she fell unconscious on his corpse.
And when she returned to life
She began to rail at herself:
"Ah! Miserable Enide!
I've killed my lord. My own
Folly has killed him. He'd still
Be alive—but stupid, arrogant
Fool that I am, I spoke
The fatal words that spurred him
To make this journey. No one's
Ever been hurt by a wise
Silence, but words do enormous
Damage: and oh, I've proved this
Over and over again."
And sitting next to her lord,
She laid her head on her knees
And began her lament once more:
"Beloved, how wronged you've been!
No one was ever your equal:
You were the living image
Of Beauty, the model of Courage;
Wisdom filled your heart;

Closed-fisted men are worthless,
But oh, how open-handed
You were! But what am I saying?
Did anyone else kill you?
It was I who uttered the words
That brought you death, my lord;
I spoke those fatal words
And I alone should be blamed.
Oh, I admit, I confess
That no one else did it:
The guilt is mine, all mine!"
She fell on the ground, senseless.
And when she awoke, she wept
And wept, on and on:
"God! What shall I do?
Why am I still alive?
Why is Death so slow,
What is he waiting for?
Even Death disdains me,
He can't be bothered. Then I
Must make amends for myself,
Take revenge for my crime:
I'll die in spite of Death,
Who refuses to help me. Weeping
And wailing will never kill me,
All my sighs are worthless.
My lord's sword, there
At his waist, deserves this vengeance.
And then I'll be in no one's
Power, beg for no one's
Assistance." She drew out his sword,
Then sat, staring at the blade.

But God in His mercy made her
Linger a little, kept her
Still. And then, as she sat,
Remembering her pain and her sorrow,
A noble count came galloping
Up, with a host of knights:
He had heard, from far away,
A lady's voice wailing.
She would have died, then
And there, but their coming surprised her:
God had not forgotten.
They took the sword from her hands,
Returned it to the sheath it had come from.
Then the count left his horse
And began to question the lady:
Who was the knight? Was she
His wife or his beloved?
"Both, my lord," she said.
"My sorrow's too great for words:
It hurts to be still alive."
Then the count began to comfort her:
"Lady, in the name of God
I beg you: have mercy on yourself!
You have reason for sorrow, yes,
But nothing deserves such misery,
For life is too good to abandon.
Don't let yourself despise it:
Take comfort, wisdom requires it,
And God will make you happy.
Your beauty's a thing of wonder,
And will bring you good fortune, for I'll
Make you my wife, you'll be

A noble lady, a countess.
That should make you feel better!
And I'll have your husband's body
Taken and buried with honor.
So stop all this weeping and wailing,
Which makes you look like a fool!"
"My lord," she answered, "leave me!
For the love of God, go away!
There's nothing here for you,
And nothing you say or do
Could possibly make me happy."
But the count turned to his knights
And said, "Quickly: make
A bier for carrying this corpse.
We'll take the body and this lady
Straight to the castle at Limors.
We'll bury it there, and there
I propose to marry the lady
(Though it's clear she doesn't want to),
For I've never seen a woman
So beautiful, nor one I wanted
So much. How happy I am
To have found her! Hurry, make
A horse-drawn bier: no
Long faces, no lazy hands!"
Some of them drew their swords,
Cut a pair of poles
From a tree, and bound branches
Across them. Then they laid Erec
On his back and hitched the bier
To horses; Enide remained
Beside it, weeping as they rode.

She fainted, often, falling
Back, but the knights who led her
Along held her upright
In their arms, and they tried to console her.
They brought the body to Limors,
To the count's palace. And all
The people who lived there trailed after—
Ladies, knights, and merchants.
They laid Erec in the largest
Room, stretched him out
On a great round table, then put
His spear and his sword at his side.
The chamber was full, everyone
Crowded around, all
Anxious to learn the cause
Of all this strange mystery and sorrow.
Meanwhile, the count called
His barons to a private council.
"Gentlemen," he said, "I plan
To marry this lady at once.
You can see for yourself how beautiful
She is, and well-bred: clearly,
She comes from some noble line.
Her grace and loveliness prove her
Worthy of all the honor
Of a kingdom, or even an empire.
My standing won't be damaged
By such a wife. Indeed,
I think it will likely increase.
So bring my chaplain here,
And some of you bring the lady,
And if she's willing to do

As I wish, I'll give her a dowry
Of half the lands I own."
Then the chaplain came, as the count
Had directed, and they brought the lady,
Too, but only by force,
For she flatly refused him. But he had
A marriage performed in spite of her,
She pleased him so much. And after
The chaplain completed the marriage,
The count's steward quickly
Prepared tables in the palace
And set out a wedding feast,
For now it was time to dine.
When evening prayers had been said,
That lovely day in May,
Enide was deeply troubled,
And nothing cured her distress,
For the count kept insisting
Sometimes politely, sometimes
Not, that she ought to smile
And rejoice. They brought her an armchair,
Which she did not want, and made her
Sit, and set a table
In front of her, like it or not.
The count seated himself
Across the table, facing her,
Growing increasingly angry
That nothing he did could please her.
"Lady," he said, "you've got
To forget this grief. Stop it!
You can count on me for all
The honor and riches you want.

You certainly know that sorrow
Won't bring a corpse to life:
It never has, and it won't.
Think of how you've been raised
From poverty's depths: you were poor,
When I found you, and now you're rich.
You've gotten a countess's rank
And honor and name—Fortune
Hasn't been stingy. True,
Your former husband is dead.
Do you think I find it strange,
Your mourning and grief? Not
A bit! But let me tell you,
For I know a thing or two,
That the moment I took you in marriage
You should have been grateful, and rejoiced.
Don't take the risk of making
Me angry. Eat when I tell you
To eat!" "My lord," she replied,
"I can't, nor will I eat
Or drink, as long as I live,
If I can't see my husband,
Lying there on that table,
Eating and drinking with me."
"Lady," he answered, "that can't
Happen. Anyone hearing
Such things would think you a fool.
Be careful, watch out! You'll pay—
And dearly—if you make me tell you
Again." She refused to reply,
Unconcerned by his threats.
So the count struck her in the face,

And she cried out in pain, at which
The watching barons scolded
Their lord: "Stop it, sir!
You should be deeply ashamed,
Hitting this lady simply
Because she won't eat. You've done
A very base thing, my lord.
Her husband lies there dead,
And this lady sees him, and mourns him,
And no one can say she is wrong."
"Shut up, all of you!" cried
The count. "She's mine, I'm hers,
And I'll treat her however I like."
Hearing these words, Enide
Swore out loud she would never
Be his, and he hit her again,
And she said, as loud as she could,
"Hah! Why should I care,
Whatever you say or do.
I'm not afraid of your threats
Or your blows. Hit me, beat me
As much as you like! I'll never
Be so afraid that I'll do
What you want, even if here
And now you put out my eyes
Or chop me to little pieces!"
  In the middle of this quarrel, Erec
Awoke from his fainting spell,
Like a man waking from a dream.
No wonder he was startled,
Seeing himself surrounded
By so many strangers, but hearing

His wife's voice raised
In despair went straight to his heart.
He jumped from the table, drawing
His sword as he came: anger,
And his love for Enide, gave him
Strength. He ran to his wife
And without a word to the count
Struck him so hard on the head
That he split it open, and blood
And brains poured out. And all
The knights leaped to their feet
And fled, convinced that the devil
Himself had attacked them. Young
And old they ran, frightened
Out of their wits, tumbling
And falling, one on top
Of the other, desperate to escape.
The entire palace emptied
Into the courtyard, no one
Too weak or too strong to flee:
"Run! Run! The dead man
Has risen!" They pushed and shoved
To the doors, too frightened to care
What happened to anyone else:
Those in the back fought
To get to the front. So clawing
And crying they got out as best
They could, and no one waited.
Quickly, Erec snatched up
His shield and hung its strap
Around his neck; Enide
Then took his lance, and together

They, too, went out in the courtyard.
But no one was bold enough
To face them, for they all believed
Erec was a body but not
A man, and the fiend inside him
Was after them. They ran,
One and all, and Erec
Pursued, chasing them
Until he came to a boy
Leading a horse, his horse,
Still saddled and bridled, to the stable.
It was almost too good to be true!
He ran straight to the horse
And the terrified servant released
The reins and ran for his life.
Erec leaped in the saddle,
And Enide, following her husband's
Instructions, set her foot
In the stirrup and jumped up ahead,
Riding in front of him, the horse
Bearing them both, she
On the neck, he in the saddle
Behind. The gate was open,
And no one dared to stop them.
It was the count's castle, and everyone
In it mourned him, but none of them,
Not even the bravest, had the courage
To seek revenge for their lord
And master, killed at his own
Table. Carrying his wife
Away, Erec embraced her,
Kissed her, murmured comforting

Words and held her hard
Against him, near his heart:
"My sweet sister, I've tested
You in a hundred ways.
Be afraid of nothing, now:
I love you better than ever,
And I understand, at last,
How perfectly you love me.
Let me, once again, be
As I was before, your servant
In everything, yours to command.
Whatever you may have said
Against me, I hereby forgive
And forget, with all my soul."
And he kissed her, and hugged her, again.
Nor was Enide displeased,
Finding herself so well
Beloved, so kissed, so embraced.
They galloped into the night,
Happy to ride in the clear
Bright glow of the shining moon.
But the news traveled even
Faster, for nothing can move
So quickly. Guivret the Dwarf
Had heard how a knight, mortally
Wounded in the forest, died,
And his lady, so lovely that Iseult
Would look like a servant beside her,
Wept and sobbed and mourned.
Count Oringle of Limors
Had found them, and carried away
The corpse, and wanted to marry

The lady, but she'd refused him.
Guivret took no pleasure
In this news, for he well remembered
His own adventure with Erec.
The thought came to his heart
To seek out the lady and if
The corpse was truly Erec
To lay him in the ground with all
Due honor. He gathered a thousand
Knights to lay siege to the castle:
Should the count be unwilling to surrender
The corpse and the lady, Guivret
Intended to burn down his castle.
Helmets laced, spears
And shields ready, he led them
To Limors, by the light of the moon,
All of them armed to the teeth.
Just before midnight, riding
In the other direction, Erec
Saw them and thought himself
Betrayed, taken captive
Or dead. He set Enide
Down near a row of hedges;
The concern he felt was hardly
Strange! "Stay here, my lady,
Behind these bushes, until
These men go by: let them
Be unaware of you,
For I've no idea who
They may be or what they want.
Perhaps there's nothing to fear,
But if we needed to keep

Ourselves safe from their weapons,
I can see no way. Whatever
I'm facing, evil or good,
Fear won't stop me from meeting
These men in combat. If any
Among them attack me, there'll be
No problem, I'll give as good
As I get, though my heart is heavy,
And my body. It's hardly surprising.
I'm riding out to meet them;
You stay here, and stay quiet:
Be careful no one sees you;
Keep silent, and let them pass."
And then, from a distance, they saw
Guivret approaching, his lance
Lowered. Neither knew
The other, for just at that moment
A dark cloud covered
The moon. Erec was bruised
And weak, but the dwarf had fully
Recovered, his wounds had healed—
What folly might Erec commit,
Not knowing the newcomer's name?
He galloped out from behind
The hedge, and Guivret charged
Straight at him, without a word,
And Erec, too, stayed silent,
Believing in the strength he no longer
Possessed, unable to admit
His weakness or allow himself
To rest. They rode at each other,
But though it looked like combat,

One was weak and the other
Strong. Guivret hit him
So hard that Erec went rolling
Backward across his horse
To the ground. Hidden in the hedge,
Enide watched her husband
Falling, and was sure he was dead;
Hurrying out, she ran
To help him as best she could.
Her grief greater than ever,
She came to Guivret and took
His horse's reins in her hand.
"Knight, may you be cursed!"
She cried. "This man was alone
And weak, in pain and almost
Dead. It was wrong to attack him,
Not knowing why or who
He was. Had he been healthy
And met you, here, alone
And unaided, you'd live to regret
The day! Be noble, now,
And generous: give up, for courtesy's
Sake, this combat you've
Begun, for you've nothing to gain,
No fame and no renown,
Killing or taking captive
A knight who can't resist you.
See for yourself: he's suffered
So many blows, been wounded
So badly, he's covered with blood."
He replied, "You've nothing to fear,
Lady! I see what a loyal

Wife you are; you have
My praise. None of my men
Will harm you, nor will I.
But tell me, don't keep it hidden,
Your lord's name. You've nothing
To lose. Tell me who
He is and you both will be safe.
I assure you, lady, neither
He nor you has a thing
To fear." Reassured,
Enide answered at once,
Wasting no words: "I'll tell you
No lies, I can see you're a loyal,
Generous knight. His name
Is Erec." Overwhelmed with joy,
Guivret dismounted and threw
Himself at Erec's feet,
There where he lay on the ground.
"My lord," he said, "I was coming
Straight to Limors, to seek you,
And thought I'd find you dead.
The news I had was that Count
Oringle of Limors had carried
Away a knight killed
In battle and meant to force
The dead knight's lady, found
Beside the body, to become
His wife. But the lady, I was told,
Disliked him. I came to her aid
As quickly as I could, and had
The count refused to hand me
You and the lady both,

I'd have thought myself a worthless
Creature to leave him one stone
On top of another. But I'd never
Have meddled in his business, except
For the great affection I feel
For you. I'm Guivret, your friend,
And any harm I've done you,
Believe me, came from not knowing
Who you were. Your pardon,
My lord!" Hearing these words,
Erec sat up, he could do
No more: "But you're excused,
My friend! You did not know me;
I forgive you your error." Guivret
Helped him to his feet, and Erec
Told him how he'd killed
The count as he sat at his own
Table, then reclaimed his horse
In front of a stable, as the count's
Men, knights and squires
And all, ran up and down,
Shouting, "Run! Run!
The dead man himself is after
Us!" And he told him he could
Have been captured, but wasn't, and how
He made his escape. And Guivret
Replied, "My lord, I have
A castle nearby, nicely
Set in a fine location.
For your pleasure and profit, let me
Lead you there, tomorrow,
So we can heal your wounds.

My two sisters, gracious
And smiling ladies, are good
Nurses; they'll cure you quickly
And well. For tonight, we'll make
Camp here in these fields,
For a bit of rest will do you
A world of good. That's my
Advice: stay here for the night."
Then Erec said, "I agree."
So they pitched their tents and remained
Where they were—which wasn't easy,
Though no one minded, for there wasn't
Accommodation for so many:
Most of them slept under
The hedges. Guivret had
His own tent put up and ordered
Kindling lit, for light
And comfort; then traveling chests
Were opened, and candles brought out,
And the tent illuminated.
And Enide was sad no longer,
For things had turned out well.
She herself took off
Her husband's armor, and his battle
Dress, then washed and cleaned
His wounds, and bandaged them,
Allowing no one else
To touch him. And Erec could find
No fault, for he'd thoroughly tested
And proved her love, and his own.
And Guivret treated him
Extravagantly well,

Laying embroidered quilts
Across a heap of the softest
Grass and flowers, to fashion
A great high bed for Erec
To lie on, piled with covers.
And then he had them open
Another chest and bring out
Three meat pies. "My friend,"
He said, "eat a bit
Of these cold pies, and drink
Some wine with water. I've seven
Barrels full, but pure
Wine will do you no good,
With all your wounds. My good
Sweet friend, try to eat,
It will do you good—and you,
My lady, who've suffered so much
Today, eat with your husband.
You've both been well avenged,
You're safe, you're out of danger,
So eat, now, my good
Friends, and I'll eat with you."
Then Guivret sat beside him,
Along with Enide, who was deeply
Pleased with everything Guivret
Had done. Each of them coaxed
Erec to eat, and gave him
Wine with water, knowing
The unmixed drink was too strong.
Erec ate as sick people
Eat, and drank a little,
Afraid to drink more, but then

He lay back, at peace, and slept
The whole night long, for everyone
Near him was careful and made
No noise. They all awoke
At dawn, and readied themselves
For a day of riding. Erec
Was far too fond of his horse
Even to think of riding
Another. Enide, who had lost
Her gentle palfrey, scarcely
Missed it (or so it appeared),
Jogging lightly along
On a borrowed mule with an easy
Gait, who carried her well.
And her heart was light, too,
Seeing how cheerfully her husband
Rode, saying he would soon
Be well. By nine that morning
They came to Penuris,
A beautiful castle, strongly
Built, where both of Guivret's
Sisters had chosen to live,
For they loved the location. And there,
In a pleasant, comfortable, airy
Room, far from all noise,
Guivret housed his guest,
And his sisters, at his request,
Set themselves to heal him.
Erec was so sure of their love
And skill that he put himself
In their hands. And first they cut
Away the dead skin, then spread

On ointment and bound the wounds
With linen. They worked hard,
As they had to; his was a difficult
Case. They washed the wounds
Often, and applied more ointment,
And gave him food and drink
Four times a day, or more,
Withholding all garlic and pepper.
Visitors came and went,
But Enide was always near him,
For no one's concern could equal
Hers. Guivret came often,
Forever alert for anything
That might be missing or wrong:
Erec was carefully, cheerfully
Tended, for no one minded
Serving so fine a knight,
But helped him gladly, of their own
Free will. The young sisters
Worked so well that in fifteen
Days his sickness and pain
Were gone. Then, to bring back
His color, they bathed him, for no one
Could teach them much about medicine;
The art was one they had mastered.
And finally, when Erec was able
To come and go as he pleased,
Guivret gave them clothes
Of two kinds of silk, specially
Sewn, the first lined
With ermine, the second with squirrel.
And one of the silks was Chinese

Blue, the other was striped
And had come from Scotland, sent
As a gift by Guivret's cousin.
The oriental blue
And ermine robe went
To Enide, the striped one, lined
With squirrel, to Erec, who would
Have been happy with either. And now
Erec was restored to health,
Healed, and as strong as ever,
And Enide was full of joy,
Her happiness restored:
They lay together at night,
All her pleasure renewed.
And her beauty, too, returned,
Replacing the drawn pallor
Inflicted by so much suffering.
Now she was hugged and kissed,
Now she had all her joy
And all her delight. They lay
Together, unclothed, in a single
Bed, kissing and hugging,
And nothing in the world could have pleased them
More, after all the misfortune
And disaster they'd known. He
Was hers, and she was his;
They had done their penance, they had paid.
Each of them sought to outdo
The other in giving pleasure:
I'm not permitted to say more.
Their love was reaffirmed,
Their great sorrow forgotten,

Almost removed from memory.
And now it was time to go home,
So they asked Guivret for permission
To leave, he who had been
So good a friend, doing
Everything anyone could do,
Serving and honoring them both.
And Erec said, when they spoke
Of parting, "Lord Guivret, I need
To go home, I can wait no longer.
Let preparations be made,
And everything needed be ready:
I should like to leave tomorrow,
In the morning, as the sun comes up.
Staying with you this long,
I will leave you healthy and strong.
May God let me live
Long enough to see you
Again and give me the chance
To do you honor and serve you.
I expect nothing will stop me
(Unless I'm captured or delayed)
From returning at once, straight
To King Arthur's court, whether
The king's at Quarrois or Carduel."
And Guivret promptly answered,
"Lord, you won't travel
Alone, for I'll come with you,
And lead you back to your king
And companions, all glad to see you
Once more." Erec agreed,
Declaring that all should be

Exactly as Guivret wished.
Everything was readied that night,
For they wanted no further delay:
Baggage and armor and horses
And all. And when they awoke,
At dawn, their horses were saddled
And waiting. Before departing,
Erec went to the sisters'
Room, to take his leave,
And Enide went with him, wonderfully
Pleased, seeing horses
And everything ready. Erec,
A well-bred man, said
Farewell to the sisters, and thanked them
For both his health and his life,
Offering them both his service.
He clasped hands with the lady
Near him, as Enide did
With the other, and then they left
The room, all of them holding
Hands, walking to the courtyard
Where the ladies' brother was waiting,
Anxious to be gone. And Enide,
Too, was more than ready
To ride. A richly prepared
Palfrey, gentle, strong,
And careful, awaited her, worth
No less than her own (which was still
At Limors), standing, patient,
In front of the mounting stone.
Hers was bay, this one
Was sorrel brown, and its head

Was totally different, as if
Designed in two parts, one cheek
The purest white, the other
Black as a barn owl, and between
The white and black was a line
As green as any leaf
On a vine. Let me tell you
About the harness and breast strap
And saddle, all magnificently
Worked. The harness and breast strap
Were studded with emeralds. But the saddle
Was completely different, covered
With dark silk. And the saddle
Bows were ivory, on which
Were sculpted the entire story
Of Aeneas fleeing Troy
And how, in Carthage, Dido
Joyfully took him to her bed,
And Aeneas deceived her, and on his
Account she killed herself,
And Aeneas went on to conquer
Laurentum and Lombardy,
Where he ruled for the rest of his life:
Subtle sculpture, finely
Chiseled, garnished in gold.
The Breton craftsman who'd made it
Had worked for more than seven
Years and done nothing else.
Whether he sold it or not
I don't know, but he should have gotten
A truly noble reward.
And receiving so fine a replacement

For her other horse left Enide
Feeling no sense of loss.
The palfrey she rode on, now,
Was so richly equipped that she climbed
To the saddle gaily, and lords
And squires quickly mounted,
Too. To cheer their journey,
Guivret had ordered a host
Of falcons and hawks brought
Along, some young, some molted,
And hounds, and hunting dogs.
They rode from morning to late
Afternoon, on a straight road,
For thirty Welsh leagues or more,
Until they found themselves
In front of a beautiful castle,
Surrounded by fine, new-made
Walls. And around their base
Ran a deep stream, rapid
And loud, rumbling like a storm.
Erec stopped to watch,
Wondering who it might be
Was lord of such a rich
Castle, and if anyone ever
Saw him. "My friend," he asked
Guivret, who rode beside him,
"Do you know the name of this place
And who rules it? Is it
A king, or a count? Tell me,
Please, since you've brought me here."
"My lord," was the answer, "I know it
Very well indeed.

The castle is called Brandigan,
And it's strong enough to stand
Against a king or an emperor.
Even if all of France,
And Lombardy, too, and everyone
From here to Liège besieged it,
They could spend their lives waiting
And never win, for it's built
On an island more than fifteen
Leagues across, containing
Whatever a wealthy castle
Could ever need—grain
And fruit and wine, and all
The wood and water they could want.
No one could starve them out,
And there's no weakness in those walls:
King Evrain built them,
Who's ruled here from the day
He was born and expects to rule
Till the day he dies. And yet
This fortress was never built
Out of fear; he's afraid of no one.
He liked the way it looked—
For take away the walls
And the towers, leave just the water
Running so fast and hard,
And why should he fear anyone?"
"God!" said Erec. "What wealth!
Let's visit this fortress, and find
Lodgings in the town around it.
I want to see this place."
"My lord," said Guivret, much

Disturbed, "please, if you don't
Mind, let's not stop:
This castle has evil customs."
"Evil?" said Erec. "Really?
Can you tell me what they are?
I'd be very happy to hear."
"My lord," said Guivret, "I'm afraid
You might be seriously harmed.
I'm well aware of your courage,
And your strength and goodwill. If I told you
All that I know of these customs—
And they're more than dangerous, worse
Than miserable—you'd be tempted to try them.
I've heard it said, and often,
That no one's attempted the deed
In seven years, or even
Longer, and come back alive.
Knights from many lands
Have tried it, brave men and strong.
Don't think I'm joking, my lord:
Indeed, whatever I know
You'll never learn it unless,
In the name of the love you've pledged me,
You swear you won't attempt
What can bring you only shame
And death." Erec had heard
Enough. "Don't worry yourself,"
He answered. "But let's at least
Seek lodgings, my good sweet friend:
It's time we put up for the night.
I've no interest in causing
You pain; but if I win

Honor in there, you'll be pleased.
I ask you only the name
Of this adventure: that's all.
Tell me that, and no more."
"How can I help myself?"
Guivret replied. "What you want
To hear, you'll hear. The name
Is delightful: it's only the deed
That's full of terror, for no one
Has ever survived it. Since
You insist on knowing, my lord,
The adventure's name—and it's sweet
Enough—is 'Joie de la Cort.' "*
"My God!" said Erec. "I hear
Good, not evil, in Joy.
And Joy I'll seek. Don't try
Changing my mind, good friend,
About this or anything else.
Let's find our lodgings, and see
What wonderful things await us.
How could anything keep me
From seeking Joy?"
"My lord,"
Said Guivret, "May God hear you
And help you find your Joy
And return as lightly as you leave!
You mean to try it, I can see.
And since it can't be helped,
We'll go: in any case,
Our lodging's already arranged.

*Joy of the Court

It's said that any knight
Of high standing who enters
This land need never seek
A bed, for King Evrain
Will be their host, and none
Will be turned away. He's published
A ban: if a merchant offers
Lodging to a traveling knight
He'll be put to death. Honoring
Men of valor is a charge
The king takes on himself."
   And so they rode to the castle,
Past wooden barriers and over
The bridge. And then townsfolk
Came out of their houses, gathered
In crowds, staring at Erec,
And seeing how handsome he was
Were sure that everyone with him
Could only be his servants.
They studied him, amazed.
The town shook with excitement,
Everyone talking at once.
Even little girls
Playing in the street stopped
Their singing and dancing, and gaped.
Every eye was on
Erec; his great beauty
Caused them to cross themselves
And raise an amazing lament:
"Oh God!" they murmured, each
To the other. "Alas, alas!
This knight who's riding by

Has come for Joie de la Cort.
How sorry he'll be, if he ever
Returns, for no one comes
From foreign lands, seeking
Joie de la Cort, and escapes
Shame and pain: they all
Pay with their heads." And then
Louder, so Erec could hear,
They called, "May God protect you,
Knight, and keep you from harm!
You're as handsome as a man can be,
And so we mourn your beauty,
For tomorrow we'll see it vanish.
Death comes for you
Tomorrow; only God
Can save you." Erec heard them,
Seven thousand voices
Raised, along the length
Of the town, but he wasn't worried.
He rode on through, not stopping,
Cheerfully greeting every
Man he passed, and they
In turn saluted him.
Many stood there, trembling
In fear, convinced they would see him
Either dead or disgraced.
Simply seeing his face,
His beauty, and how he carried
Himself won their hearts,
Men and women and girls,
All dreading the suffering and pain
He would feel. And King Evrain

Heard how a knight was approaching
His court, leading a large
Troop of men; to judge
By their weapons and armor their chief
Was a count or perhaps a king.
Evrain set himself
In the middle of the road, and called out,
"Greetings! Welcome to all
This company, and their lord and master!
Welcome, gentlemen. Please
Dismount." They dismounted, and many
Willing hands led off
Their horses. Seeing that Enide
Was with them, the king behaved
With great correctness, greeting her,
Then quickly helping her down.
Leading her by her soft
And lovely hand, he brought her
To his palace, as courtesy required.
And there, thinking no evil
Thoughts, nor anything foolish,
He offered her honor, knowing
Full well what honor was.
He had incense lit
In that room, and myrrh and aloe,
So that everyone, entering, praised
The king's manners. And Evrain
Led them in, hand
In hand, exceedingly happy
To have them. But why should I tell you,
In immense detail, all
The paintings and silk drapery

Beautifully hung on the walls?
Why waste our time on foolish
Matters when what I really
Want is to speed things up?
Drawing my story straight on
Is better than dragging it off
The road. So I won't delay.
When the hour for dinner arrived,
The king ordered it served.
(Nor will I linger here,
For I see a straighter path.)
Whatever they wanted, whatever
They liked, was there to be eaten:
Fowl and venison and fruit
And many varieties of wine.
But best of all was the good
Company—for the sweetest dish
On the table is always pleasant
Talk and smiling faces.
It all went gaily and well
Until, abruptly, Erec
Stopped eating and drinking,
Remembering why he was there:
The Joy he was hunting came
To mind, and he turned their talk,
And the king let him lead the way:
"My lord," he said, "it's time
I said what was on my mind
And why I've come here. I've already
Waited too long to speak;
I can't keep silent any longer.
I claim Joie de la Cort,

There's nothing in the world I want
So much. Whatever it is,
Please let me have it, if you can."
"Sweet friend," said the king, "you couldn't
Have spoken stupider words.
This is a horrible business:
Many good men have suffered.
And you yourself, when it's over,
Will be dead and torn apart
Unless you take my advice.
Believe me, do as I say:
I ask you to withdraw your request
For this ghastly affair, which you can't
Finish; it will bring you no good.
Say no more! Be silent!
Only an utter idiot
Would disregard this counsel.
I'm hardly surprised, finding you
Anxious for fame and honor,
But to see you taken captive,
Or beaten, wounded, and bleeding,
Would cut my heart to the quick.
Please understand me: many
Brave men have come here, claiming
A right to this Joy, but none
Have ever won it; each
And all are dead and gone.
Tomorrow, just before dark,
You, too, can make the attempt,
You, too, can have this Joy,
But you'll pay a terrible price.
It's not too late, you can still

Withdraw, repent and retreat
In your own best interest. I tell you
These things because to tell you
Less than the whole truth
Would be to betray you." Listening
To the king's words, Erec
Was aware what good advice
He'd been given, but greater danger
And wilder wonder only
Made him want the thing more!
So he said, "My lord, I see
You're a brave and loyal knight.
I couldn't possibly lay
Any blame on you, if I make
This attempt, no matter what happens.
The wheel's been spun, the dice
Have been cast—and in all my life
I've never flinched or pulled back,
Once I've begun, until
I've done the best I can do."
"I understand only
Too well," said the king. "You mean
To seek Joy despite
What I've said. But you make me despair,
For the end is bound to be bad.
Still, you have my pledge,
I'll give you whatever you need.
And if you succeed in winning
Joy, you'll gain honor
Greater than any man
Alive has ever known.
May God in His goodness give you

Joy to bring back with you."
  All night long they talked
Of nothing else until,
Their beds prepared, they went
To sleep. Erec awoke
As dawn was breaking, saw
The sun's clear light and, rising
From his bed, began to make ready.
But Enide, tortured with doubts,
Awoke in anguish. Seized
The whole long night with fear
And suspicion, she'd worried for her lord,
So willing to face this peril.
And here he was, preparing
Himself, and no one could stop him.
The moment they'd risen, the king
Had sent him the weapons and armor
He would need, and Erec accepted,
Knowing how badly used,
All battered and broken, his own
Equipment had become. Delighted
With his host's generous help,
He prepared himself for battle.
And when he was ready, he left
The great hall, walking
Down flights of stairs to where
His horse, saddled and bridled,
Awaited him, and the king, already
Mounted, was also waiting.
The whole court was waiting,
And all the townsfolk, too:
No one in castle or town,

Man or woman, tall
Or short, straight or bent,
Strong or feeble, wanted
To miss it; all came, if they could.
And as they began to ride,
A swelling roar rolled
Along the streets, everyone
Calling, peasants and nobles
Alike: "Ah ha, knight!
Joy has betrayed you. You dream
Of conquest, but all you'll get
Is pain and suffering and death."
Every one of them shouted,
"God has cursed this Joy,
It's killed many brave men!
And today, without any doubt,
It will do its worst!" Erec
Was listening carefully, hearing
Everything said, right
And left: "How you've been wronged,
Brave knight, so noble, so good!
No, there's no justice
Leading you to this early
Death, to where you'll find
Wounds and suffering and pain."
He heard it all, every
Word, but kept on his way,
Never lowering his head,
Showing no sign of fear.
No matter what, it was time
He saw and understood
Whatever it was that frightened them

All, gave them such pain.
  The king led him out
Of the castle, past the town,
Straight to a garden nearby;
And all the people trailing
After prayed that God
In His mercy might let him leave
With Joy. And I, despite
My weary tongue, cannot
Omit a true description
Of this garden, as history records it.
  There were no walls around it,
No fences, but only air:
It was sealed by black magic at every
Point by invisible air,
Shuttered tight, as if
By bars of iron. The only
Entry was a single gate.
Inside, flowers blossomed,
Summer and winter, and fruit
Ripened—but bore a spell
That let it be eaten only
There in the garden; no one
Who tried to carry it out
Would ever succeed, unable
To find the only gate
Unless they put back what they'd taken.
Every bird that flies
Through the air, delighting, rejoicing
Men with its song, could be heard
In that garden, and more than one
Of each kind. And the ground itself,

As far as the eye could see,
Grew rich with every herb
And spice men use for medicine,
Every root and leaf.
   Everyone entered the same
Narrow gate, King
Evrain first and the rest
After. Erec, his lance
Ready in its rest, rode
To the middle of the garden, relishing
Birds singing them countless
Songs of Joy—Joy,
Which more than anything else
He longed for. And then he saw
An astonishing thing, able
To frighten the most famous of knights,
Old Thibaut the Esclavon,
Or those we know better today,
Ospinel or Fernagu:
For there in front of them, impaled
On spikes, was a row of gleaming
Helmets, and under every
Helmet but one was a head.
The last spike, they could see,
Held nothing except a horn.
Whatever this meant, Erec
Had no idea, but none of it
Made him afraid; the king
Rode at his right hand,
So he asked Evrain to explain.
And the king replied: "My friend,
You don't understand the meaning

Of this thing we see in front of us?
You ought to feel mortal fear,
If you value your life, for this one
Empty spike, where only
A horn hangs, has been waiting
For a knight. Who? We don't know—
You, or someone else.
Be careful, don't let the head
Be yours, as it's meant to be.
Don't forget; I warned you,
Before you entered here.
I doubt you'll ever come back,
Except as a headless corpse.
And since you know, now,
This spike awaits your head,
Then understand that if,
As predicted (as soon as this
Was set in the ground, hung
With a horn), your head is there,
Another spike will be planted,
And it, too, will await
A head, though God knows whose.
I've nothing to tell you about
The horn, for no one's been able
To play it, but whoever can
Will earn the greatest honor
And fame of any knight
In this land: he will become
Knight of all knights across
The world, honored everywhere.
There's nothing more to be said:
Have your people fall back,

For in just a moment Joy
Will arrive, and bring you sorrow."
  And King Evrain left him.
Erec bent down to Enide,
Who was weeping bitter tears,
Nor was it sorrow that kept her
Silent, for the sadness you speak
Means nothing: it's the heart that matters.
But knowing her heart well,
He told her, "My good sweet sister,
My noble lady, loyal
And wise, I know your heart,
I see its fear, which you feel
But don't know why. But you frighten
Yourself for nothing. Unless
You see my shield shattered
And a blade pierce my body—
Unless you see my gleaming
Mail shirt bathed in my blood,
My helmet cracked and broken,
And me stretched on the ground,
Beaten, defeated, unable
To defend myself, forced
To beg for mercy, and await it,
Helpless, against my will
—Then you can wail in sorrow.
You've started too soon. My sweet
Lady, neither you
Nor I know what this is.
You terrify yourself
For nothing—for let me tell you,
All the courage and strength

I have comes from your love,
And with it I can face, hand
To hand, any man living.
I may be a fool to say this,
But it isn't pride speaking,
Only my need to comfort
You. Feel better! Let
It be! And now I must go,
And you can't join me, I'm forbidden
By the king's own orders to lead you
Any farther." And then
He kissed her, and commended her
To God, and she him,
But a deep sadness fell
On her heart, knowing she couldn't
Stay with him, follow him, and see
With her own eyes what
This adventure might be and how
He would deal with whatever it was.
Since she couldn't go, she stayed,
Sad and sorrowing. And he
Went down a winding path,
Alone, none of his men
With him, and found, under
A sycamore tree, a silver
Bed, covered with gold
Brocade, and on the bed
Was a young woman, as beautiful
As beauty could be in both face
And body, sitting alone.
What more can I say, except
That simply seeing her beauty,

The delightful way she was dressed,
Would make you swear, truly,
That even Aeneas' wife,
Lavinia of ancient Laurentum,
Noble and lovely as she was,
Had barely a fourth of her beauty.
Erec went closer, wanting
To see her better, then seated
Himself at her side. And then
He saw a knight under
The trees in that garden, wearing
Bright red armor, a man
Incredibly tall, and except
For his size he'd have seemed the handsomest
Man on earth, but he towered,
According to every knight
Who'd ever seen him, at least
A foot above all other
Men. And even before
Erec saw him, he began
To shout, "Knight! Knight!
So help me God, you're crazy:
How can you dare approach
My lady? By my soul,
You aren't worth enough
To come anywhere near her.
By the eyes in my head, you'll pay
Dearly for this stupid behavior.
Get away!" Then he stopped
And stared at Erec, who never
Moved. And so they stood,
Motionless, until Erec

Decided to speak his mind.
"My friend," he said, "words
Of folly and sense are equally
Easy. Threaten as much
As you like; I'll listen, but I won't
Reply. No man who makes threats
Understands anything. Would you like
To know why? A man persuades
Himself he's won, and then
He loses. A threatening, over-
Confident man is a fool.
Some men run, some men
Chase. But I'm not so afraid
Of you that I'll run: here
I stand, ready to defend
Myself if anyone wants
To attack me. If you're looking for a fight,
I promise you I'm prepared."
"As God is my witness," he answered,
"You won't need to worry! I challenge you,
Knight! Here and now
I defy you!" Need it be said
That after this they held back
Nothing? No little lances
Were used, but large ones and solid,
And the wood well dried, to make it
Stiff and strong. They struck
Each other's shining shields
Such blows that the sharp points
Dug holes deep enough
For a man to stand in, but never
Reached as far as the flesh,

And neither spear cracked.
And then, as quickly as they could,
They pulled their lances out
And, as the rules require,
Threw themselves back into combat.
Fiercely determined, they struck
Such powerful blows that, this time,
Each of their lances shattered
And their horses sank to the ground.
But the men sitting in those saddles
Were strong and quick on their feet,
And neither was hurt, but leapt
Safely away. And then,
In the middle of the garden, they stood
On two legs and swung their heavy
Swords of Viennese steel,
Smashing tremendous strokes
Against the gleaming shields,
Splintering them into pieces.
How their eyes glittered
And burned! Were there any way
To do each other more damage,
They'd have struggled to find it, first
Trying the cutting edge
Of their swords and then the flat,
Hammering away at cheeks
And helmet nose guards, at the hands
Holding swords, at arms,
At temples, necks, and collar-
Bones, until they ached
All over. Weary and in pain,
Instead of stopping, they drew

On reserves and redoubled their efforts.
It was hard to see, for all
The sweat, mixed with blood,
Dripping into their eyes.
Their blows began to miss,
As happens when men no longer
See where their swords are swinging.
No matter what they did,
Neither could kill the other—
But have no fear, they tried
As hard as they could. Sight
Completely gone, unable
To see a thing, they dropped
Their useless shields and fought
Fiercely, slowly beating
One another down
To the ground, on their knees. And still
They fought, on and on,
Until it was after noon
And the tall knight grew
So tired he couldn't breathe.
Erec dragged him up
And down, shook him so hard
That his helmet laces broke
And he tumbled to the earth, falling
Flat on his face, unable
To get up, incapable of movement.
No matter what it cost him,
He was forced to admit defeat:
"You've won, you've beaten me—
But oh, how hard to confess it!
Still, perhaps it's not

As bad as it might be: you may be
Someone so famous that defeat
Is respectable. So tell me truly,
Please, if I'm permitted
To ask, your name, for there may be
Comfort in the knowledge. Let me
Assure you, I'd never be sorry
To be beaten by a better man.
But if I've been conquered by someone
Less well-known than myself,
My sadness would be overwhelming."
"My friend, I'll be glad to tell you
My name," said Erec. "Of course!
You'll know before I leave
This place, provided you tell me,
First, what you're doing
Here in this garden, and why.
Tell me the whole story,
Including your name, and the nature
Of this Joy. I'm impatient to hear it."
"I'll tell you everything," the other
Answered, "exactly as you wish,
With nothing omitted." Then Erec
Decided to reveal his name.
"Have you ever heard," he asked,
"Of a king named Lac and his son,
Erec?" "I have, my lord.
Before I became a knight
I spent a great many days
At that king's court; were it up
To him, I'd never have left it."
"Having been so long

At the court of King Lac, my father,
You ought to know me well."
"My God, what good luck!" he exclaimed.
"Now let me tell you why
I've lingered so long in this garden.
And I'll tell it all, exactly
As you asked, no matter how painful.
That girl sitting over there
Was my childhood love, and I
Was hers. Our love for each other
Matured and grew still greater,
Until she asked me to give her
A gift, but wouldn't say what.
Who could deny his love
A gift? No courteous lover
Could refuse her any pleasure:
He's obliged to oblige her, without
Hesitation, as best he can.
So I said I would, of course,
But she said she also wanted
My solemn oath. So I swore it
And offered anything else
She might like, but my oath was enough.
I'd promised, but didn't know what
Until she told me I would be
Her knight. My uncle, King
Evrain, dubbed me a knight,
Here in this garden, in the presence
Of many brave men. And then
The lady revealed my oath
And explained what it meant: I would never
Leave this garden until

A knight came and conquered
Me in battle. Either
I stayed in this garden or broke
My pledge to the lady, although
I'd never known what she wanted.
But once I saw what the dearest
Creature in the world craved,
What choice did I have? I've done
My best to pretend I approve,
Since once she knew I didn't
Her heart would never be mine
Again—and God knows nothing
Could make me let that happen.
Which is how my lady has kept me
Here, all these years,
For she couldn't believe anyone
Would ever come along
Able to challenge and defeat me.
And thus she thought she could easily
Hold me captive, here,
For the rest of my life. And how wrong
I'd have been, having whatever
Strength and skill I possess,
If I hadn't defeated knights
I was able to beat in combat:
Escaping that duty would only
Be proper for a peasant! I couldn't
Shirk that task, not even
For the dearest of friends. I always
Wore my armor and carried
My weapons, and never refused
A challenge. You've seen the helmets,

You know how many knights
I've conquered and killed. Was I wrong?
All things considered, no—
I couldn't help myself,
Unless I chose to be false
And disloyal and break my oath.
I've told you the whole truth:
Do understand, the honor
You've won is no small affair.
And you've brought an immense Joy
To all my friends and my uncle's
Court, for now I can leave.
And since this Joy you've released
Pleases everyone at court,
They'll call it Joie de la Cort—
And oh! how long they've awaited
This Joy, restored to them only
By you, you who have fought for
And won it. Whatever magic
And spells you've used to defeat me,
Bewitch away my strength,
You've earned the right to know
My name, which you've asked me to tell you.
My name is Mabonagran,
Though no one wherever I've lived
Knows me by that name or will think
It sounds familiar, for I've used it
Only in this land. No matter
How hard they've tried, no one
Anywhere else has learned it.
This, as I say, is the truth,
My lord, as you ordered it told.

But still, there's one thing more.
I believe you've seen the horn
Hanging on an empty spike.
I'm not permitted to leave
This garden until it's been sounded,
And then I'll truly be free
And Joy will begin, since anyone
Hearing that horn, who knows
Its secret, is thereby enabled,
In spite of any obstacle,
To attend my uncle's court.
So rise, my lord, and quickly
Fetch that horn, for now
There's nothing to keep you from doing
What you need to do." Erec
Rose at once, and the beaten
Knight rose with him, and together
They went in search of the horn.
And Erec blew it, and blew
It loud, and its voice carried
Far and wide. And hearing
That sound, oh, what happiness
Enide felt! And Guivret,
Too, rejoiced. And King
Evrain and all his people
Were delighted: every single
Soul was filled with such pleasure
They couldn't stop singing
And dancing and making merry.
Erec could surely have boasted
That no one had ever created
Such Joy. Who could describe it?

No human mouth would know how—
But let me try, briefly,
Without too many words.
News of the great adventure
Flew across the land,
And nothing could keep the whole
World from coming to court,
People flocking from every
Side, on foot and on horse,
No one willing to wait.
Meanwhile, those in the garden
Removed Erec's armor,
All of them trying to sing
The best song to celebrate
Joy. And ladies composed
A poem, and called it "The Song
Of Joy"—a poem, alas,
Now lost. And Erec was well fed
With Joy, exactly as he wished.
But the lady seated on the silver
Bed was less than over-
Joyed with the Joy she saw;
It brought her little pleasure.
How often we're forced to suffer
The sight of what tears at our heart!
But Enide was a wellborn lady,
And seeing how sad and somber
The girl sat, all alone
On her bed, decided to approach her,
Asking in courteous fashion
Who and what she was,
And perhaps to tell her story

If it wasn't too painful. Enide
Intended to approach her alone,
Taking no one with her,
But many of the noblest, most beautiful
Ladies and girls, seeing
Where she went, followed along,
For friendship and affection, and wanting
On their own account to comfort
A lady so seriously saddened
By Joy. And the cause of her sadness
Was this: it seemed to her
That once he left the garden
She'd never see her beloved
As much as she had before.
But she knew her displeasure made
No difference: he would have to leave,
The time had come, her terms
Had been met. Which was why she wept,
The tears wetting her face.
She was sadder and more afflicted
Than I know how to tell you, but like
A lady she rose to greet them,
Even seeing that no one
Approaching was likely to ease
Her pain or staunch her sorrow.
Enide greeted her sweetly,
But for a long time there was no
Response, wracked as the girl
Was by tears and sobs.
Finally, she managed to return
The greeting—and then she stood
Silent for another good while,

Staring hard at Enide,
Thoughtful, as if she knew her,
Had seen her before and remembered
Her face, but couldn't quite
Be sure. And then, taking
Heart, she asked Enide
Where she was from, the name
Of her country, and where her husband
Had been born. Enide answered
At once, telling the truth:
"I'm the niece," she said, "of the count
Who rules in Laluth. My mother
Was born his sister. And I
Was born and raised in Laluth."
And then the girl laughed
Hard and long, so delighted
At what she'd heard that, clearly,
Her sorrows suddenly meant
A good deal less to her. The joy
In her heart leaped and danced,
Nothing could hide it. She came
And hugged Enide, and kissed her,
Saying, "I'm your cousin.
That's the honest truth.
You're my father's niece,
For he and your father are brothers.
I think you've never heard
How I come to be here;
No one has told you. The count—
My father, your uncle—had a war
To fight and hired soldiers
From many lands. And as

It happened, my lovely cousin,
The king of Brandigan's nephew
Came there, with one of those knights,
And stayed with my father for a year.
That was, I believe, twelve years
Ago. I was only a child,
And he was handsome and charming,
And so we agreed, we two,
That we would be married when we could.
I wanted only whatever
He wanted, and he wanted me,
Pledging to love me forever
And be my beloved, and bring me
Here to his home, a plan
That pleased us both. It was hard
To wait, hard for us both;
We longed to be together.
So finally we did come,
Though no one knew it. In those
Days, you and I
Were only little girls.
And that's my story. Now tell me,
Exactly as I've told you,
Just how it happened that your lover
Came to know you." "My lovely
Cousin, we were married
With my father's consent, and my mother's,
Too; they were both pleased.
Both our families knew,
And rejoiced, as they ought to. The count,
My uncle, was truly delighted,
For my husband's so worthy a knight

That no one could find a better,
And now there's no need for him
To prove his strength or his skill,
For where is the knight so young
Who could be his equal? He loves me
Very much, and I love him
More; no love could be greater
Than ours. I've always known
I loved him, I couldn't doubt it;
He's a king's son,
And he took me, threadbare and poor,
And brought me more honor
Than anyone so disowned
As I was has ever known.
And if you like, I'll tell you
The whole story, truthful
In every detail, of my rise
To these heights. I love to tell it!"
And then she told how Erec
Had come to Laluth, hiding
Nothing, telling the entire
Adventure truly and well,
Omitting nothing. But I
Don't dare tell it over
Again, for nothing's duller
Than a twice-told tale. And as
They talked together, one
Of the ladies rose and went
To tell the assembled barons
How truly wonderful their Joy
Had become. And they all agreed,
Hearing her words, and rejoiced,

But Mabonagran was the gayest
Of all, hearing that his lovely
Lady was happy once more.
Even the lady who'd hurried
To bring him the news found
Herself rejoicing. And King
Evrain rejoiced with them,
For happy as they'd been, before,
Now they were happier still.
Enide brought her beautiful
Cousin—more beautiful even
Than Helen, and better bred,
And more charming—to meet her husband.
Everyone rushed to join them,
Mabonagran and Guivret,
And King Evrain, all
Greeting and being greeted,
Each honoring all
The others, no one holding
Back. Mabonagran
Delighted Enide, and she
Him. Erec and Guivret
Took great pleasure in the girl
From the garden; they hugged and kissed
Each other freely. And then
They talked of returning to the castle,
For they'd stayed too long in the garden.
They readied themselves to leave,
And the king himself led them
Out, still rejoicing,
Kissing and hugging each other,
But before they came to the castle

They encountered lords and barons
From every part of the land:
Whoever had heard of their Joy,
And was able to come, was there.
The crowd was enormous, all
Trying to greet Erec—
High and low, poor
And rich, everyone bowing
And calling greetings and saying,
Over and over again,
"God save the man who brought
Joy back to our court!
God save the most fortunate man
He in His wisdom ever
Created!" They led Erec
To court, showing their joy
In whatever ways they could.
Harps could be heard, and fiddles,
Playing every sort
Of song and dance, all
The instruments anyone could name.
But I need to sum this up
More briefly: I'm taking too long.
The king lavished honor
On Erec, and every knight
At court offered, with open
Hearts, to serve him. Their Joy
Lasted for three whole days;
Then Erec was able to think
Of home: on the fourth day
He was ready to leave, despite
Their prayers. He left with a joyous

Escort, a crowd of knights:
Saying farewell to them all,
If he'd made the attempt, would
Have taken another half day.
The barons hugged and hailed him;
He commended the others to God,
Saying farewell to one
And all. Nor was Enide
Silent, in bidding the barons
Goodbye: she greeted them all
By name, as they did her.
And in taking leave of her cousin,
She gently kissed and hugged her.
They were gone. The Joy was over.
Knights rode in every
Direction. Erec and Guivret
Galloped happily off,
Straight to the castle where Arthur,
They'd been told, was staying. The king
Had been bled the day before;
He was in his private chambers,
Accompanied, now, by only
Five hundred knights of his household.
Arthur had never been
So alone, whatever the season,
And it left him depressed, having
So few at his court. Just then,
A messenger came from Erec
And Guivret, riding rapidly,
To announce that his masters were hurrying
To Arthur, with their men following
Behind. Coming to the king

And his knights, with great courtesy
He greeted them: "My lord, Erec
And Guivret the Dwarf have sent me."
And then he told them how soon
His masters would arrive. The king
Answered: "Such brave and noble
Barons are always welcome!
I've no better knights than these two:
My court will be much improved."
And then he sent for the queen
And told her the news. Courtiers
Rushed to saddle their horses,
Hurrying so hard to greet
The newcomers they couldn't take time
To buckle on their spurs.
Let me tell you, just
As quickly, that the travelers' lesser
Servants had already reached
The town—lackeys and cooks
And pages—to prepare their masters'
Lodgings. But the others were still
On the road, though some were close
To town and some had begun
To arrive. They were greeted as they came,
Kisses and hugs were exchanged.
Then they went to their lodgings, removing
Road-worn clothes and, at
Their leisure, dressing in their finest
Robes. And when they were ready
They came to court, where the king
And queen warmly welcomed them,
Especially anxious to see

Erec and Enide. The king
Seated them close to his side,
Kissing Erec and then
Guivret. He hugged Enide
And covered her with kisses.
Nor did the queen hold back,
But embraced Erec and Enide,
Happy as a lark high
In the air and singing merrily.
Everyone welcomed them back.
Then the king called for quiet
And, turning to Erec, requested
An account of his new adventures.
When all were silent and still,
Erec began his tale,
And told them the entire story,
Omitting nothing. I hope
You're not expecting me
To go back and tell it all
Again? Hardly, for you know
Exactly what he did,
And why; I've just finished
Telling you. To do it again
Would be painful, and not particularly
Brief, so why start over,
Rehearsing all his words
Just as he said them—the tale
Of the three knights he defeated,
And then five more, and the count
Who tried so hard to disgrace him,
And then the giants he'd killed.
Erec marched his way

Along the story, one foot
After the other, and got
To the count, cut down as he sat
At his dinner, and told of finding
His horse once more. "Erec,"
Interrupted the king, "remain
Here, stay at my court,
As you used to." "My lord, if that
Is what you wish I'd gladly
Stay here a year, or two,
Or even three, but ask
Guivret to stay, if you please,
And I'll ask him myself, as well."
The king made the request,
And Guivret agreed. And so
Both remained at Arthur's
Court, as the king had wanted,
For he loved and honored them both.
Three of them stayed at the court,
Erec, Guivret, and Enide,
Until Erec's father,
A very old man, died,
And the barons, all the noblest
Men in the realm, had messengers
Seek Lac's son, and finally
Found him at Tintagel,
A week before the Nativity.
They told him exactly how
His old father, snowy
Haired, had left this life
Behind. Erec was deeply
Saddened, but had to hide

His sorrow, for a king's pain
Is indecent, if public: it needs
To be kept from ordinary men.
Erec had vigils and masses
Chanted at Tintagel;
He made vows and redeemed
Golden promises made
To hospitals and churches.
And he did what he ought to do,
Choosing more than a hundred
And sixty miserable paupers
And giving them all new clothes,
And to priests, and many poor men
In sacred orders, he gave,
As he should, new hats and warm
New cloaks. For the love of God
He did good, giving sacks of pennies
To those who needed them. And after
Sharing his wealth, he showed
His wisdom, asking and receiving
His kingdom from Arthur's own hands.
And then he asked the king
To let him be crowned at home.
And the king told him to be ready,
For he and his queen would be crowned
Together, both at once,
On the day of Christ's Nativity,
Adding, "I'll plan to crown you
At Nantes, in Brittany,
And there you'll assume the royal
Insignia, a crown on your head,
A scepter in your hand. And thus

I'll honor you." Erec thanked him
For so gracious a gift. The Nativity
Came, and the king summoned
All his barons, without
Exception, and ordered their ladies
To come with them. Not
A one stayed home. And Erec
Had sent for many noble
Knights, but even more
Came than he'd ever expected,
Wanting to serve and honor him.
Nor can I name for you those
Who came—and as for those
Who didn't, it makes no difference.
Erec was careful to include
His wife's father and mother:
Indeed, he asked them first
Of all, and they came richly
Dressed, like proper rulers
Of a castle, accompanied not
By priests, who got to stay home,
Or fools and gawkers, but good knights
And those who were dressed to the hilt.
Every day they traveled
Far, joyously enduring
The long journey, reaching
The city of Nantes in time
For Christmas Eve. Nor did they
Pause but immediately went
To the lofty, noble room
Where Erec and Enide, awaiting
Them, hurried to kiss

And hug the newcomers without
Delay, happy to greet them
Sweetly, as they well deserved.
Having made their guests welcome,
They took them by the hand and joyfully
Led them before the king
And queen, who were seated together;
They greeted the host and his wife
Graciously. Standing hand
In hand with his wife's father,
Erec declared: "My lord,
Here is my host and good friend,
Who did me the great honor
Of making me lord of his household.
Before he knew who I was
He offered me handsome lodgings,
Gave me whatever he had,
And without consulting a soul
Even gave me his daughter."
"And this lady with him, my friend,"
Said the king, "who is she?"
"My lord, the lady of whom
You speak is my wife's mother."
"Her mother?" "Indeed, my lord."
"Ah, I can certainly see
That a flower culled from a plant
So lovely must itself be a beautiful
Bloom, and be noble, and its fruits
Lovelier still, for goodness
And beauty spread like perfume.
Enide is beautiful, as in reason
And justice she'd have to be,

With a mother so exceedingly lovely
And a father so good a knight.
"She's bred true to her line,
For in all her principal features
She closely resembles her parents."
The king had finished, and was silent.
He ordered Enide's parents
To be seated; without a word
Of protest, they obeyed at once.
Enide was enormously happy,
Seeing her father and mother
Again, for she had not seen them
In a very long time. Whatever
Might happen now seemed
Good, and pleased her so much
That although she showed her happiness
Freely, the joy she felt
Was greater than the girl could express.
But that's enough of that:
What interests me more, at the moment,
Is the nobles gathered at Arthur's
Court from countries all over
The world, counts and kings
From Normandy, Brittany, Scotland,
And Ireland; England and Cornwall
Produced a horde of rich barons,
And Wales as far as Anjou,
And Maine, and Poitou. No knight
Of noblest rank, no great
Lady, charming and gracious,
Had stayed away: all
The noblest and best came to Nantes

As their mighty king had commanded.
Please, listen carefully:
Once they had all assembled,
Before the bell for evening
Prayers had rung, Arthur,
Anxious to augment his court,
Dubbed more than four hundred
New knights, sons of kings
And counts, gave each three horses
And three pairs of new robes.
The king was powerful and open-
Handed: it wasn't woolen
Cloaks he gave them, or mere rabbit
Fur, but satin and ermine,
Adorned with squirrel and brocade,
Heavy with golden trim.
Even Alexander,
Immensely rich and generous,
Conqueror of all the world,
Seems stingy and poor in comparison!
Not Caesar, emperor of Rome,
Nor any of the kings named
In all the tales of chivalry,
Could have given a banquet like the one
King Arthur gave on the day
Erec was crowned, and neither
Caesar nor Alexander
Would have dared to spend as much
On feasting as was spent that day.
Cloaks had been taken from storage
Chests and left, lying
Free for the taking, in every

Room; no one was watching,
Or minded. Gleaming British
Sovereigns had been sprinkled on a cloth,
Right in the middle of the court,
For those were the days of Merlin,
And British coins were everywhere.
Everyone was fed, that night,
From the king's kitchens, carrying
Quantities of food to their lodgings.
In the middle of the morning, that Christmas
Day, everyone gathered.
The vast joy that was coming
Flooded Erec's heart.
Yet no one, no matter how skilled
In the art, could tell you, in any
Human tongue, a third,
Or a fourth, or a fifth, of all
That took place at that coronation.
I've taken on a fool's
Task, trying to describe it,
But since the responsibility
Is mine, and I must attempt it,
Let me do the very best
I can with my limited ability.
  Two brand-new chairs, fashioned
Of brilliant white ivory, both made
Precisely the same, had been set
In the hall. Clearly, the craftsman
Who'd carved them had been clever and subtle,
For in height, and length, and breadth,
And in decoration, no matter
How you looked, or where,

You saw them exactly the same:
No one could possibly tell
One from the other. And every
Piece in each of those chairs
Was either ivory or gold,
Chiseled with a delicate touch,
The two front feet sculpted
Like a pair of leopards, and the back ones
Like crocodiles. They were gifts
Of homage and respect for Arthur
And his queen, given by a knight
Whose name was Brian of the Islands.
  Arthur sat in one
And Erec, wearing a robe
Of rich black silk, was seated
In the other. The robe was described
In a book I read, written
By Macrobius, who taught the science
Of attentive vision: I mention
His name to prove I'm telling
The truth. I draw the details
Of the cloth from his pages, exactly
As I found them there. It was woven
By four fairies, working
As great and masterful craftsmen.
And the first had spun an accurate
Portrait of Geometry and how
It measures sky and earth,
Capturing every aspect—
Including depth and height,
And length and width, and how
We follow the sea from shore

To shore, measuring its width
And depth: in short, measuring
The world. That was the first fairy's
Work. The second spun
A picture of Arithmetic,
Carefully tracing the steps
By which we count days,
And the hours they're made of, and count
Every drop in the ocean,
And each tiny grain of sand,
And all the stars on high,
And how many leaves on a tree,
And how we frame these numbers—
All accurately counted,
Employing no tricks and no lies,
For this fairy knows what she weaves.
And her subject was Arithmetic.
The third chose to show Music,
Which blends with every human
Pleasure, in counterpoint
And song, with harps and lutes
And viols—a beautiful picture,
With Music seated and in front
Of her her tools and delights.
But the fourth and final fairy
Drew the noblest portrait,
Having chosen the highest art:
Astronomy, which governs
And regulates marvels, the stars
In the sky, and the moon, and the sun.
And in every respect it rules
Entirely by its own arts,

Independently sure
Of whatever it needs to do,
Knowing whatever has been,
Perceiving whatever is still
To come, its learning precise,
Containing no lies and no fraud.
The fairies embroidered these things
In golden thread, on the cloth
From which Erec's robe was made.
And the lining was sewn from the skins
Of strange and wonderful beasts,
Their heads pale and blond,
Their necks dark as a mullet,
Their spines red, their bellies
Mottled, and their tails blue.
They come from the Indies, they're called
Berbiolettes, and they eat
Aromatic spices,
Fresh cloves and cinnamon.
What can I tell you about
The cloak? It was lush and beautiful,
With four gems for its clasps:
Chrysolite green on one side,
Amethyst purple on the other,
And all mounted in gold.
　And still Enide had not yet
Come to the palace; seeing
She was late, the king instructed
Gawain to go and lead her
There at once. Gawain
Hurried to obey, taking
With him King Carduant

And the generous king of Galway,
Plus Guivret the Dwarf, and also
Ydier, King Nudd's son.
And other barons quickly
Joined them, to escort the ladies:
There were more than a thousand—enough
Good knights to conquer an army!
The queen had been busy, making
Enide ready, and now
She was led to the palace by courteous
Gawain on one side, and the generous
King of Galway on the other,
Who cherished the girl, and no wonder,
For Erec was his nephew. When they reached
The palace, who hurried out
To greet them but Arthur himself,
And then, in a courteous display,
He seated her next to her husband,
Wanting to do her great honor.
And then he ordered his servants
To take a pair of heavy
Gold crowns from his treasure chests,
And they rushed to obey his commands,
Quickly returning with massive
Crowns of gold, embossed
With great red rubies, each of them
Boasting four rich stones,
And even the smallest burned
With a light many times brighter
And clearer than the moon. And those
In the palace who looked at that light
Were unable, for some considerable

Time, to see at all.
The king himself was dazzled
By the brilliant glow, but rejoiced in it
All the same, delighting
That the gems shone so beautifully
Clear. Two girls presented
The first crown, two barons the other.
Then Arthur ordered his bishops
And priests, and his monastery
Abbots, to come and anoint
The new king, according to Christian
Law. And every man
Of the cloth, whether young or old,
Hurried to obey him—and you know
There were plenty of priests at court,
And abbots, and bishops. And then
The great bishop of Nantes,
A truly holy man,
Beautifully consecrated
The new king, and placed
The crown on his head. King Arthur
Ordered a wonderful scepter
Brought out, which all admired.
Listen and hear how this scepter
Was made: it glowed like a bell glass,
For it was set with a single emerald
As fat around as a fist.
And let me tell you the truth:
No fish that swims in the water,
No wild beast, no manner
Of man or flying bird,
But the artist had cut and worked

Its image into the stone.
They brought the scepter to Arthur,
Who stood a moment, admiring it,
And then with no further delay
Placed it in King Erec's
Right hand, making him a proper
King. Then he crowned Enide.
They were summoned to Mass, and went
To church, there to hear
Mass and attend the service,
Then prayed at the bishop's palace.
Enide's father and mother
Could be seen crying for joy.
To tell you the truth, his name
Was Licorant, and hers
Was Tarsenfide, and both
Were extravagantly happy. The procession
Reached the bishop's palace,
And the monks from the monastery
Came rushing out, bearing
Sacred relics and treasures,
Holy books, and crosses,
And incense holders, and coffers
Containing the bodies of saints,
Of which there were many. They hurried
To meet the procession, chanting
As they came; there was no shortage
Of singing. So many kings
And counts and dukes and barons
Had never attended Mass
All at the same time.
So many had gathered that the chapel

Was full to bursting; only
Ladies and knights could get in;
And common people stayed out.
But even many noble
Knights waited outside
At the door, for so many had come
That the chapel could not hold them.
After the Mass had been heard
They all returned to the castle,
Where preparations were complete,
Tables set up and covered—
At least five hundred, or more.
Yet how can I dare describe
What you won't believe? Five hundred
Tables in a palace hall?
You'd think me a colossal liar.
But it's not what I said: they filled
Five rooms, not one, and packed them
So tight you could hardly move.
Every table boasted
A king or a count or a duke,
And every table seated
At least a hundred knights.
A thousand knights in brand-new
Ermine robes brought bread,
And a thousand wine, and a thousand
Meat. All sorts of dishes
Were served: I could name them for you,
Every single one,
But more important things
Need to be said: they ate
As much as they wanted, freely

And exceedingly well, were graciously,
Joyously served, and were happy.
The banquet over, Arthur
Said farewell to all
The assembled kings and dukes
And the many, many counts,
And all the others, including
Ordinary folk, who'd come
To the feast. And because he loved
Erec, and it was right that he do so,
He gave them gifts of horses,
Weapons, money, and many
Kinds of beautiful cloth.
And that's the end of the story.

Afterword

Joseph J. Duggan

Erec and Enide, thought to have been composed around 1170, is the earliest romance of King Arthur. Other romances in French preceded it, but they were devoted to figures and events taken from the Greek and Roman past (the fall of Troy, Aeneas, Oedipus, Alexander the Great). As an educated man, and probably a cleric, Chrétien would have been familiar with these romances of antiquity. He refers to Alexander in several places and has the story of Dido and Aeneas carved on Enide's saddlebows in ll. 5332–42. He also alludes to the story of Tristan and Yseult, which would be the counter-text for his second romance, *Cligès,* and to the Latin writer Macrobius, author of the *Dream of Scipio.* A native Welsh Arthurian prose tale, *Culhwch and Olwen,* precedes *Erec and Enide,* perhaps by as much as a century, and scattered references to Arthur are found in earlier Welsh texts. But although Chrétien was a prolific user of Celtic lore and oral tradition, he seems to have had no direct knowledge of any surviving work of Celtic literature—and in any case the Arthur presented in *Culhwch and Olwen* has none of the qualities of courtliness associated with him in the French tradition.

The connection of Arthur with courtliness, and in fact his

fame in Europe outside Celtic lands, results from Geoffrey of Monmouth's *History of the Kings of Britain* (ca. 1136), an astonishingly successful work that blended folk and historiographic traditions to establish Arthur as the paragon of kingship. Geoffrey, prior of the Abbey of Monmouth and a teacher at Oxford, claimed that his account was translated from "a very old book in the British language," probably what we would call Welsh, though it may have been Breton. (Speakers of Welsh and Breton could understand each other in this period.) His intent was to attribute to the kings of Britain a history that traced back to a prestigious event of ancient times, the fall of Troy, and he posited their descent from Aeneas's great-grandson Brutus (Geoffrey claimed that this explained why they were called "Britons"). In Geoffrey's history, Brutus leads his people to the island later named for him, founds London, and gives rise to two lines of descendants, one in Britain and one in Brittany. When the first of these royal branches dies out, the people have recourse to the second, naming Constantine II of Brittany their king. Constantine's son Uther Pendragon and eventually his grandson Arthur succeed him. Arthur defeats the Saxons in a series of battles that culminates in a great victory near Bath. During a twelve-year peace, Arthur develops a code of courtly demeanor that inspires nobles, even those in distant parts, to imitate him and his knights. He then conquers other lands, including Ireland, Norway, Denmark, and, after a nine-year campaign, Gaul. Another period of peace ensues, during which Geoffrey shows Arthur holding a magnificent court in Wales at Caerleon, the City of the Legions, attended by Hoel, leader of the Bretons, and the twelve peers of Gaul. When word comes that the procurator of the Roman Republic, Lucius, demands homage, Arthur leads a large army onto the Continent, leaving his wife, Guinevere, and his nephew Mordred in charge of the kingdom. Although many of Arthur's men, including the knights Kay and Bedevere, die in battle, Arthur is nearing victory against the Romans when he learns that Mordred has seized the throne of Britain and is living in adultery with Guinevere. Returning immediately, the king and his men meet Mordred's forces in a series of battles at Richborough (where Gawain, depicted at different points as Arthur's cousin or nephew, is killed), at Winchester, and finally at a site on the River Camblam, where Arthur kills Mordred but is "mortally" wounded and transported to the island of Avalon so that his wounds can be healed.

The periods of peace during which, according to Geoffrey, Arthur was able to devote himself to courtly pursuits gave Chrétien the narrative pretext for his Arthurian romances. In fact, Chrétien nowhere mentions Mordred or the Battle of Camblam, let alone Mordred's relationship with Guinevere, and he refers only in passing to Arthur's counselor Merlin (see l. 6697), whose prophecies are the subject of book 5 of the *History of the Kings of Britain.* Instead, Chrétien concentrates on the adventures of Arthur's knights, for which the king himself provides a backdrop of exemplary sovereignty and stability. The idea of the Round Table seems to have come to Chrétien from Wace, a Norman poet who translated Geoffrey's history into French as the *Roman de Brut* (*Romance of Brutus*), perhaps for Eleanor of Aquitaine, in about 1155. The catalogs of those present at Arthur's court when Erec and Enide arrive there and of those who attend the couple's wedding are repertories of the possibilities at Chrétien's disposal, and several of these characters, including Gawain, Lancelot, Yvain the son of Urien, Kay, and Gornemant, reappear in his other romances. Melwas, lord of the Island of Glass, figures later as Méléagant, the villain of *Lancelot: The Knight of the Cart.*

As the first Arthurian romance, *Erec and Enide* includes features that audiences came to expect in other works of its type: an opening at Arthur's court at Cardigan (or Cardiff, or Caerleon . . .) on a major Christian feast day; the mention of Arthur, Gawain, and the Round Table; the anticipation that, before the feast begins, an opportunity for high adventure, often associated with some custom, will present itself; a focus on the loves, warrior exploits, and changes in fortune of the knights rather than of Arthur himself; tests of prowess against seemingly superior and sometimes preternatural challengers; and, last, a resolution accompanied by a ceremony that betokens stability. Some of these traits are also found in lays, relatively brief episodic poems composed, like *Erec and Enide,* in rhymed couplets, of which the earliest surviving examples are Robert Biket's *Lay of the Horn* and the lays of Marie de France.

Erec and Enide shares with another of Chrétien's romances, *Yvain: The Knight of the Lion,* a concern with possible conflicts between the contentment of wedded life and the demands of knighthood. In both works, the first section consists of an adventure that leads to the knight's marriage, which in turn gives rise to a questioning of his reputation for chivalric prowess. Stability is achieved only in the second part after a series of adventures leads to a reconciliation between husband and wife. At stake above all is the knight's renown, not so much what he thinks of himself as what others think of him. A lowering of esteem leads to public shame, which robs the knight of his reputation. The reestablishment of his worth in the eyes of his fellow nobles is a central theme of each romance.

In *Erec and Enide,* news of what people are saying about Erec—namely, that his preoccupation with his surpassingly beautiful bride has led him to neglect chivalric duties—reaches his ears through an inadvertent remark by Enide. Erec's reaction is sudden and harsh: on his orders, Enide hastily prepares to leave Arthur's court, with no escort but Erec and with no fixed destination. But Chrétien, who in other contexts is fond of revealing the inner lives of his main characters, leaves the reader in the dark about his hero's intentions. In forcing Enide to ride quickly ahead of him in her best dress and on her finest horse, but in total silence, does Erec want to punish her for doubting his prowess? Or for lying to him in ascribing his overhearing of her words to a dream? He appears to be setting her out as bait for robber knights, such as the two groups that soon attack. Enide is surely being tested, but is it a test merely of devotion or also of chastity? Chrétien tells us what Enide is thinking, but his silence on the issue of Erec's purpose is masterful, compelling the reader to speculate on the character's motivations. There can be no doubt, however, that Erec is purposely exposing Enide to danger as well as placing himself at risk by defending her far from the protection of court.

Before Erec and Enide are reconciled in their moonlight ride, each is put to the test many times. Erec wins out in successive battles against first three and then five predatory knights, the lustful count (called Galoain in most manuscripts) and his hundred followers, the little king Guivret, two giants, and Count Oringle of Limors. Enide warns him about the robber knights and the lustful count, nearly kills herself when she thinks Erec is mortally wounded, and rejects Count Oringle's proposal of marriage. She demonstrates her faithfulness in part by violating his prohibition against speech. She also comes to appreciate his prowess fully.

The episode of Guivret, little king of a group of Irish followers, is curious and makes one wonder if it once circulated as an independent adventure about an encounter with a king of the *síde,* or fairy-mounds. In spite of his small stature, Guivret fights from tierce to none, at least six hours by the modern clock, until Erec at last breaks his sword. The battle seems to occur for no particular reason, and ends in a pact of friendship. Later Guivret, not recognizing Erec, and intending to rescue Enide from Count Oringle, again battles Erec. On learning Erec's identity, Guivret gives Erec over into the care of his two sisters, skilled healers who put him on a pepper- and garlic-free diet. Arthur, too, has a sister, Morgana le Fay, who produces unguents in both *Erec and Enide* and *Yvain;* and whose healing skills are applied to the "mortally" wounded Arthur at the end of the thirteenth-century anonymous prose romance *The Death of King Arthur.*

Chrétien calls the culminating adventure "Joie de la Cort" (Joy of the Court), in accordance with the medieval predilection for deriving a name from its contrary: only when the ordeal is done away with will there be joy in the court. Guivret acts as a guide, leading Erec to the castle of Brandigan and explaining the wonders of its garden to him. Mabonagran, the knight whom Erec must meet in single combat, has been constrained by his lover to fight all challengers who approach her in this garden of perpetual summer. The relationship between Mabonagran and the damsel is the opposite of Erec and Enide's. Whereas Erec and Enide married with the knowledge and consent of all their kin, Mabonagran and his lady (who turns out to be Enide's cousin) eloped. By this point in the narrative, Erec and Enide are bound to each other in a relationship of mutual respect and affection. But Mabonagran's lady, fearing that he will leave her when the Joie de la Cort ends, has bound him in captivity through a "rash boon"—in this case, his prior consent to grant her whatever she demands. By contrast, Erec's victory over Mabonagran confirms the exemplary nature of his marriage to Enide. It also expresses a principal theme of the romance, the proper balance between devotion and freedom of action, achieved only through measured conduct.

But the episode of Joie de la Cort, in which Welsh mythological characters' names are embedded, has another, mythic sense that is harder for us to grasp. Mabonagran is the avatar of the divinity Maponos (Welsh "Mabon"), son of Matrona (Welsh "Modron"), the great Celtic mother goddess for whom the River Marne is named. His uncle in the romance, Evrain, lives in the castle of Brandigan, the first syllable of which is the name of another Celtic deity and mythological king, Bran the Blessed. In the Irish *Voyage of Bran,* this figure visits, among other places, an Isle of Joy. A horn is one of Bran's attributes. Roger Sherman Loomis has proposed that "Joie de la Cort" was a garbling of "Joy of the Horn" (Old French *corn*), a remnant of which would be the magic horn that Erec blows to end the enchantment. Bran's horn, in fact, was a horn of plenty, supplying food to the point of satiation, and it is surely not coincidental that after Erec blows the horn Chrétien describes him as "well fed with Joy" (ll. 6198–99). One conjecture reads the name "Mabonagran" as a combination of "Mabon" and "Bran." An attribute of Mabon and his counterparts in medieval Welsh tradition is to be a prisoner, and Mabon's liberation from captivity is one of the tasks Arthur's men undertake in *Culhwch and Olwen.* Although the mythological significance of the story on which Chrétien based the Joie de la Cort episode is obscure, that it was a tale incorporating elements of Celtic myth is certain.

The adventures with which *Erec and Enide* opens are also of Celtic provenance. In Irish and Welsh mythology, sovereignty is represented by a woman whom the man aspiring to kingship must win and marry. Erec wins Enide in the Test of the Sparrowhawk from the arrogant knight Ydier, whose father, Nudd, is the avatar of the Celtic god Nodens. The Hunt for the White Stag, a contest that Arthur both revives and wins, gives him the right to kiss the most beautiful woman in the court, Enide. The kiss also signifies, however, that Enide is a figure of sovereignty. In keeping with this status is her association with horses, a quality she shares with Rhiannon (the goddess Rigantona, "Great [or Divine] Queen") in the collection of Welsh mythological tales known as the *Mabinogi.* Enide takes care of Erec's horse when he first arrives in Laluth. Her cousin presents her with three horses as she leaves for Arthur's court. She watches over three horses that Erec captures, then five more. Her ordeal, like that of Rhiannon in two tales of the *Mabinogi,* is associated with horses. Her reconciliation with Erec takes place as they ride off on a single horse. Finally, she receives from Guivret a horse whose head is half white and half black, with the two colors separated by a green band, a combination suggesting otherworldliness.

The clothing of Erec and Enide takes on heightened significance in light of their progression toward sovereignty. At Erec's insistence, Enide is led to Arthur's court in tatters. There Guinevere gives her a new tunic and cloak, reinforcing the notion that, like Arthur's wife, Enide is an embodiment of sovereignty. When after the crucial bedroom scene Erec orders Enide to precede him through the forest, she is to ride on her best saddle horse in her most beautiful dress, presumably to attract the attention of malefactors. Just after the lovers are reconciled, Guivret has two beautiful robes made for them, indicating, I believe, that they love each other equally. In the Christmas coronation scene at Nantes, in Arthur's presence, Erec is crowned wearing a silk robe made by four fairies. On its inner lining are portrayed fabulous Indian beasts that feed on cinnamon and cloves. On the exterior is depicted the quadrivium, the four liberal arts that involve measurement—geometry, arithmetic, music, and astronomy—which would be especially appropriate for a king to know in order to rule effectively. The robe appears to symbolize that Erec no longer has to prove his prowess or honor and is now finally shown to be without equal. The acquisition of the qualities that render a man and a woman fit to rule a kingdom is, then, a major thematic thread of *Erec and Enide,* interwoven through the text and symbolized by their association with luxurious clothing.

Where would Chrétien have gotten the Celtic material that plays a major role in this poem? He tells us at the beginning of the romance that others usually ruin the adventure story on which he is basing his work. These "others" were likely to have been Breton storytellers, famous in the twelfth century, who entertained audiences in many parts of western Europe with tales of Celtic origin. A certain Bleri, who is said to have known stories about all the kings and counts of Britain, is cited by several medieval authors as the link between Celtic tradition and Continental poets. Bleri is purported to have visited the court of Poitiers, perhaps when William of Aquitaine, the earliest known troubadour, was count. He may be the "Bleri the translator" who is attested as being in charge of a Norman castle near Carmarthen in 1116. Although this would be too early for direct contact with Chrétien, the name "Bleri" seems to be recalled under an altered form in l. 1698 of *Erec and Enide.* The names of Erec and Enide provide further clues. According to Rachel Bromwich, they appear to come from Breton tradition; she points out that there was an area of Brittany known as Bro Wened ("land of the Veneti, territory of Vannes" but easily misinterpreted as "land of Ened" or "Enide") and also as Bro

Gueroc ("land of Gueroc" or "Erec," after a fifth-century ruler). This seems to indicate that Chrétien's main sources were Breton rather than Welsh or Irish.

In any case, Chrétien boasts of having made of his source (or sources) an adventure tale that is beautifully constructed and, punning on his name, will last as long as Christianity (ll. 24–25). (And, in fact, we are still reading it eight hundred years later.) The term *adventure* in stories associated with the matter of Britain connotes a sense of expectation. The knight (and in this romance his lady as well) puts himself at the mercy of fate, wandering through forests in which danger awaits him, often in the form of otherworldly creatures that threaten him both physically and morally.

But *Erec and Enide* is not merely a good story; it is a story that holds up the actions of the eponymous couple as, in the end, exemplary. Erec and Enide, the accomplished knight and the surpassingly beautiful young woman, have found their way through crisis and adventure to a point at which they not only have sound reasons to trust each other but are fit to rule a kingdom. The theme of the relations between a noble couple in love and the society that surrounds and calls on them dominates the poem. These relations, though tested, are maintained successfully by Erec and Enide, but are not handled successfully either by Ydier and his lady or by Mabonagran and Enide's cousin until Erec forces both couples to end their isolation. The development of this model fulfills the implied promise Chrétien made at the beginning of the romance when he wrote that some things are worth more than they at first appear: his tale is not merely entertaining but edifying.

Like other writers of romance and historiography in this period, Chrétien seems to have been oblivious to the vast differences in social conditions, manners, and morals that separated his contemporaries from the world of Arthur. If Arthur was indeed a historical figure, he lived in the sixth century, long before the conventions of chivalry, vassalage, and courtesy were invented. The depiction of Arthur's world in terms of the later twelfth century, although born of a lack of awareness of historical difference, facilitates Chrétien's task of showing how an ideal king might deal with his vassals. He may have been thinking of such contemporaries as Louis VII of France or Henry II Plantagenet, ruler not only of England but of most of western France (and both men married Eleanor of Aquitaine). This exemplary purpose is evident in Arthur's speech in ll. 1757–77 setting out the ideal of the just monarch who maintains the customs of the past, and his insistence in ll. 60–61 that a king's command is not to be contradicted.

Two of Chrétien's other four romances were written for well-known patrons, Eleanor of Aquitaine's daughter Marie de Champagne (for *Lancelot: The Knight of the Cart*) and Philip of Flanders (for *Perceval: The Tale of the Grail*). No patron is mentioned in *Erec and Enide.* The guests at the wedding of Erec and Enide, however, come exclusively from lands that were under the suzerainty of Henry II Plantagenet or within his sphere of influence. Moreover, the timing and place of the coronation scene, at Christmas in Nantes in Brittany, coincide with those of a court Henry held there in 1169. Chrétien's placing of the coronation at Nantes seems otherwise unmotivated, as that city does not figure elsewhere in the romance. The court of 1169 was assembled for the nobles of Brittany to swear homage to Henry's third son, Geoffrey. That same year Geoffrey took the title duke of Brittany and was betrothed to Constance, daughter of Count Conon IV of Brittany. Chrétien might well, then, have written *Erec and Enide* for Henry II or for Geoffrey (both, after all, spoke French), or for another noble in their entourage. Henry II certainly took an interest in the legend of King Arthur, and Constance named Geoffrey's posthumous son Arthur, another indication of the importance of the Plantagenet dynasty's desire to link itself with the Arthurian past. Even the mentions of Guivret king of the Irish, and of the presence of Garras, ruler of Cork, at the wedding celebration would be appropriate shortly after 1169–70, a period marked by decisive Norman incursions into Ireland.

As the earliest Arthurian romance, *Erec and Enide* exercised considerable influence on the genre. In addition, three derivations or analogues were composed in the twelfth and thirteenth centuries: the Middle Welsh *Gereint, Son of Erbin,* the Middle High German *Erec,* and the Old Norse *Erex Saga.* The last two of these fall under the rather loose rubric of translations, a category that in this period included a healthy dose of what we would call adaptation. The relation of the Welsh romance to Chrétien de Troyes's work has been a topic of controversy. Some have maintained that *Gereint* is the source of *Erec et Enide,* others that the debt runs in the opposite direction, and still others that they derive from a common source. One reasonable view seems to be that *Gereint* is based on a hearing of either *Erec et Enide* or one of its more or less immediate sources, perhaps a Breton version. The listener would then have retold the story in Welsh, incorporating in the process features that conformed to Welsh tradition but were not found in the original. Among the elements of Welsh lore—for which see Rachel Bromwich's edition and translation of the Welsh triads—introduced in *Gereint* are the central figure himself, Gereint, son of Erbin, a sixth-century ruler and traditional hero of southwest Britain, the porter Glewlwyd Mighty-Grasp, the hero Owein, Arthur's chief physician, Morgan Tud, and

Arthur's dog Cafall. Gereint's father, Erbin, is represented as Arthur's cousin. Guivret is referred to as Gwiffret Petit, but it is said that the Welsh call him the Little King. There are several notable differences in the plot. During the couple's journey, Gereint makes his wife wear her worst dress rather than her best, and Gereint's coronation takes place toward the middle of the romance rather than at its end. In addition, Gereint's motivation is more clearly expressed and quite uncomplicated: he suspects that Enide may be in love with another man.

The German *Erec,* by the knight Hartmann von Aue, is the earliest romance of King Arthur in that language, generally dated to the early 1190s. Like *Gereint,* it places the coronation after Enide first arrives in the kingdom of Erec's father. Hartmann, not understanding why Enide should be taking care of so many horses, adds an excursus on Morgana le Fay's ability to change a human into an animal and her power over wildlife, as well as one on the origins of Enide's remarkable palfrey, said to have been stolen by Guivret from a dwarf. Whereas in Chrétien's romance Erec pardons Enide for having spoken ill of him, Hartmann has Enide pardon Erec for having tested her. Having dispelled the Joie de la Cort, Erec leads to Arthur's court the eighty widows of the knights beheaded by Mabonagran in that enchantment. At the end of the tale, the happy couple find their reward in heaven.

Erex Saga was written on the basis of *Erec and Enide* for King Hákon Hákonarson of Norway, probably in the third decade of the thirteenth century, and it exemplifies still another type of reception. Although this compact tale is substantially the same, it adds two episodes not in the French: Erec's battle with a dragon and his encounter with seven armed men. Again there is no coronation scene at the end, but the royal couple is said to have two sons.

In addition to its importance in establishing the genre of Arthurian romance and its intrinsic qualities as a highly entertaining and instructive tale, then, *Erec and Enide* played an essential role in the transmission of courtly ideals from France and the Norman nobility of Britain to other parts of Europe, one of the most significant developments in the history of Western civilization.

Recommended for Further Reading

Medieval Texts

Blaisdell, Foster W., and Marianne E. Kalinke, trans. *Erex Saga and Ivens Saga: The Old Norse Versions of Chrétien de Troyes's Erec and Yvain.* Lincoln: University of Nebraska Press, 1977.

Bromwich, Rachel, ed. and trans. *Trioedd Ynys Prydein: Triads of the Isle of Britain.* Cardiff: University of Wales Press, 1978.

Burgess, Glyn S., and Keith Busby, trans. *The Lais of Marie de France.* London: Penguin Books, 1986.

Cable, James, trans. *The Death of King Arthur.* Harmondsworth: Penguin Books, 1971.

Jones, Gwyn, and Thomas Jones, trans. *The Mabinogion.* Everyman's Library. Rev. ed. New York: Dutton; London: Dent, 1974.

Raffel, Burton, trans. Chrétien de Troyes. *Yvain: The Knight of the Lion.* With an Afterword by Joseph J. Duggan. New Haven and London: Yale University Press, 1987.

Resler, Michael, trans. Hartmann von Aue. *Erec.* Philadelphia: University of Pennsylvania Press, 1987.

Thorpe, Lewis, trans. Geoffrey of Monmouth. *The History of the Kings of Britain.* Harmondsworth: Penguin Books, 1966.

Critical Studies

Bromwich, Rachel, A. O. H. Jarman, and Brynley F. Roberts, eds. *The Arthur of the Welsh: The Arthurian Legend in Medieval Welsh Literature.* Cardiff: University of Wales Press, 1991.

Burgess, Glyn. *Chrétien de Troyes, Erec and Enide.* Critical Guides to French Texts, 32. London: Grant and Cutler, 1984.

Frappier, Jean. *Chrétien de Troyes: The Man and His Work.* Trans. Raymond J. Cormier. Athens: Ohio University Press, 1982.

Gies, Joseph, and Frances Gies. *Life in a Medieval City.* New York: Harper Colophon Books, 1981. [Life in thirteenth-century Troyes.]

Kelly, Douglas. *The Art of Medieval French Romance.* Madison: University of Wisconsin Press, 1992.

———. *Medieval French Romance.* Twayne's World Authors Series, 838. New York: Twayne, 1993.

Kelly, Douglas, ed. *The Romances of Chrétien de Troyes: A Symposium.* Edward C. Armstrong Monographs on Medieval Literature, 3. Lexington, Ky.: French Forum, 1985.

Lacy, Norris J., and Geoffrey Ashe. *The Arthurian Handbook.* Garland Reference Library of the Humanities, 765. New York: Garland, 1988.

Lacy, Norris J., Douglas Kelly, and Keith Busby, eds. *The Legacy of Chrétien de Troyes.* Amsterdam: Rodopi, 1987–88.

Loomis, Roger Sherman. *Arthurian Tradition and Chrétien de Troyes.* New York: Columbia University Press, 1949.

Luttrell, Claude. *The Creation of the First Arthurian Romance: A Quest.* London: Edward Arnold, 1974.

Maddox, Donald. *Structure and Sacring: The Systematic Kingdom in Chrétien's Erec et Enide.* Lexington, Ky.: French Forum, 1978.

———. *The Arthurian Romances of Chrétien de Troyes: Once and Future Fictions.* Cambridge Studies in Medieval Literature, 12. Cambridge: Cambridge University Press, 1991.

Topsfield, L. T. *Chrétien de Troyes: A Study of the Arthurian Romances.* Cambridge: Cambridge University Press, 1981.

Uitti, Karl D. *Chrétien de Troyes Revisited.* Twayne's World Authors Series, 855. New York: Twayne, 1995.